A BATTLE AT SEA . . .

"Row!" Kirk ordered. He and Spock grabbed their oars and bent their backs to the task, while Godor kept nervously scanning the water's surface for Sealons. Had all the fishermen been with them, as Kirk had planned, they could have made good speed, but as it was, the boat moved away from the site of their primitive depth-charge with agonizing slowness.

An enormous concussion slammed the boat upwards. Kirk and Spock were tumbled from their seats onto the boards, but Godor, who had been half standing, shot out of the boat into the water. He surfaced instantly, his face filled with terror, and screamed wordlessly at them . . .

Look for STAR TREK Fiction from Pocket Books

THE TRELLISANE CONFRONTATION

DAVID DVORKIN

A STAR TREK® NOVEL

POCKET BOOKS

New York   London   Toronto   Sydney   Tokyo

Another *Original* publication of POCKET BOOKS

POCKET BOOKS, a division of Simon & Schuster Inc.
1230 Avenue of the Americas, New York, N.Y. 10020

This book is published by Pocket Books, a division of
Simon & Schuster Inc., under exclusive license from
Paramount Pictures Corporation.

ISBN: 0-671-67074-3

First Pocket Books printing February 1984

10 9 8 7 6 5 4 3

POCKET and colophon are trademarks of
Simon & Schuster Inc.

Printed in the U.S.A.

Chapter One

Captain's Log: Stardate 7521.6

Standard orbit has been established around the outpost colony on Trefolg. Due to the sensitive nature of this mission, I had planned to beam up the prisoners and return directly to Star Fleet Headquarters. However, the governor of the colony, Lerak Kepac, has issued a formal invitation to me to pay a courtesy call. This is a request I have of course agreed to honor.

Kirk thumbed the log recorder off and took a moment to look around the bridge in satisfaction. His crewmen and officers sat at their stations working with calm efficiency or walked briskly with firmness and purpose. No wonder these outpost colonies along the perimeter of the Romulan Neutral Zone felt safer, reassured, when one of the great starships stopped by. Especially, he thought with a touch of smugness, *this* starship.

The elevator doors swished open and the ship's doctor ambled in, wearing his dress uniform, and strolled over to the command chair. "Well, Jim,"

Doctor McCoy drawled. "How do I look? Good enough to impress a colonial governor?"

Kirk smiled and looked his friend up and down. No matter what uniform McCoy wore, he managed to make it look somehow crumpled, as if he had just finished a long evening of card playing while wearing it. Kirk shook his head. "It'll do. At least you're wearing your dress uniform. More important, you're wearing your old country doctor *persona*. That's just right."

"Thought it would be for a colony. Mind telling me what's up?"

Kirk stood up and stretched. "Come to my quarters. I'll have to change quickly before we beam down."

He didn't speak again until they were in his spartan cabin with the door closed. "Sorry, Bones. I didn't want to discuss it any further on the bridge." As he spoke, he stripped his uniform off quickly and chucked it into a small vent in the wall. It disappeared with a faint *swooshing* sound. He drew a fresh dress uniform with the insignia of a Star Fleet captain from its packaging and pulled it on, checking his appearance perfunctorily in a mirror. "I'm sure you know, since everyone else on the ship already seems to, that we're here to pick up some prisoners. This courtesy call on the governor I told you to dress up for is an extra. Partly it's to reassure the colonists that, even though the Neutral Zone is right ahead of them, the Federation and Star Fleet Command are behind them."

"Nice turn of phrase you have."

Kirk grinned at him. "In addition," he said, walking to the door, "Governor Kepac said he had a message he had to give me in person, something he preferred not to broadcast to the ship."

As they walked down the corridor toward the transporter room a few minutes later, McCoy remarked, "You know, Jim, it sure is nice to see you looking relaxed for a change. As if you're enjoying your job."

"Relaxed, yes." Kirk pondered for a moment.

"There's little to wear on you on this type of mission, no real tension, in spite of the kind of prisoners we're picking up. And yet," he shrugged, "I can't really say I enjoy it that much. It's—well—it's just *too* routine!"

McCoy laughed. "Okay, then. Worry about it being too routine."

Four Security guards were waiting in the transporter room, ordered by Kirk to meet them there. Sometimes he wondered how Star Fleet Security managed to keep finding new recruits; the job was probably the most dangerous on any starship. Looking at the four, all tall, heavily muscled, and self-confident, he wondered how Security managed to find so many recruits whose faces all looked alike. It was the expressionlessness that did it, along with that air of power, readiness, and competence. The answer, he knew, lay in their training, a training as long and rigorous, in its own way, as his had been; they were well equipped to handle trouble, and Kirk was confident that these four would be more than enough to handle the nine manacled prisoners waiting for him on the surface of Trefolg.

Kirk, McCoy, and the four Security guards stepped onto the transporter platform and arranged themselves on the six available positions. On the return trip, Kirk planned to use one of the cargo transporters, so that the entire group, which would then number fifteen, could beam up together. He wanted to avoid the complications of sending the prisoners up in two or more groups, splitting the group of Security guards up, and having to have more Security men sent to the transporter room to cover the prisoners as they arrived. The ship was operating smoothly and easily, with no problems; the crew calm and as relaxed as he was himself. He didn't want to take any chance of upsetting that.

Kirk spoke briefly to Chief Engineer Scott, who had come to the transporter room himself to operate the controls. He preferred to be in charge in person when the captain or any of the other chief officers, such as the ship's doctor, were beaming up or down. "Scotty, it shouldn't take more than three hours to satisfy Governor Kepac's social requirements. Have the transporter in Cargo Bay Number Two kept ready and cleared and beam up all fifteen of us there when I contact you."

"Aye."

"Whenever you're ready."

Engineer Scott moved the levers on his control panel forward, listening as he did so to the whining hum that grew in the transporter platform mechanism; he was not even consciously aware that he always did this, listening, with the instinct born of so many years' intimacy with the machinery, for any flaw in the sound, any indication that the transporter was functioning less than perfectly. The six men on the platform wavered, changed into six vague, manlike outlines composed of winking, twinkling lights, then vanished. Moments later, the Transmission Confirmed light blinked on on his panel, signifying that they had appeared on the surface of the planet below. Scott sighed and relaxed, shaking off the tension that invariably gripped him when Captain James Kirk was among those being transported.

As Scotty's square face faded away and the functional buildings of the colonial administration center on Trefolg replaced the control room, James Kirk felt his own tension rising again. Sometimes, as during the last few days, he could relax while onboard the *Enterprise,* but he felt somewhat unprotected and on guard when he left the ship's protective walls and beamed down to a planetary surface.

Governor Kepac came hurrying out of the building in front of them in person to greet the party from the *Enterprise.* He was accompanied by an aide. Kirk remembered having met Kepac some years earlier, before he had assumed the governorship of the Trefolg colony, and he remembered him as having been short, chubby, carefree, and constantly cheerful. Now Kepac was almost thin, his clothes hanging on him indicating that he had lost a great deal of weight quite recently. His carefreeness was gone, and his once-smooth face was creased with permanent worry lines. Nonetheless, he smiled broadly as he came up to Kirk.

"Captain Kirk! I'm delighted to see you again."

Kirk nodded and shook the outstretched hand. "Governor. This is Doctor Leonard McCoy, my chief medical officer. I thought you might like to have him look over your medical facilities and supplies. We might be able to provide some things from ship's stores."

"By all means. We'd be delighted. Mr. Johnson," he nodded toward the man who had accompanied him, "will show your guards where the prisoners are being kept and we can meet them there later."

There was a refreshing lack of ceremony and large groups of subordinates on these frontier colonies. After they had dropped McCoy off at the colony's main hospital—a small and primitive affair compared to the medical facilities on the *Enterprise*—Kirk and Governor Kepac were alone. "Well, Lerak, you said you had a message for me?"

They had reached a large open field beyond the buildings. Shapes, trash of some kind, were scattered all over the field. There was something familiar about the shapes that Kirk could not pin down.

"Yes," Kepac said. "I do. After Star Fleet had dispatched your ship here to pick up our prisoners, we received a coded subspace message from Trellisane. Very weak. It's only because our receivers are so powerful out here that we picked it up at all."

"Trellisane," Kirk murmured thoughtfully. He knew something of that world because of its unique and sensitive position. Could this be the trouble that the Federation had feared for so long?

As if reading his mind, Kepac said, "I don't think the worst has happened. But they did request that Star Fleet send a ship. I doubt if their transmission even reached Star Fleet Headquarters in any coherent form, so I thought I'd let you know and leave it to you." He hesitated. "I didn't want to broadcast any of this, either up to your ship or to Star Fleet, because I was afraid I'd start some sort of panic here. This colony always skates along the thin edge of panic. We're next-door neighbors to the Neutral Zone, and if the Romulans decide to start a war, we'd be the first to go."

"Of course, Lerak. I understand." Kirk thought he understood, too, why Kepac had changed so greatly over the last few years. "I hope the *Enterprise*'s presence will at least reassure your colonists that they haven't been forgotten. Now, tell me what this place is." He pointed toward the field.

"I thought you might find this interesting. Shows the length to which fanatics will go. As I told Star Fleet Command, the prisoners you're here to pick up are members of the United Expansion Party. They were about to enter the Romulan Neutral Zone, hoping to provoke a war between the Romulans and the Federation, when one of our ships intercepted them."

Kirk shook his head. "In spite of what the United Expansion Party may think, the Romulans have grown more tolerant. They wouldn't go to war over an incursion by a group of fanatics in a civilian ship."

Kepac grunted. "It was more serious than that. They had bought an old cargo ship, but they added an enormous amount of metal superstructure and plating to it so that from the outside, visually at least, it resembled a Star Fleet scout ship. They knew enough to make it look to the Romulans like a military provocation."

"But the Romulans would have known better as soon as they boarded her."

"They wouldn't have gotten the chance. The prisoners have been telling us all this quite freely, by the way. They're proud of it."

"Because they see themselves as the true patriots and you as the traitors for stopping them, I suppose," Kirk remarked.

"Exactly. They planned to put up the appearance of a fight—enough anyway to make the Romulans destroy them. Then the Romulans would have no way of knowing what they really were, and they would be convinced the Federation was planning to take over the Neutral Zone, in violation of the treaty."

"They would have died when the Romulans destroyed their ship!"

"Of course. No price too great to pay. All of this in front of us," he swept his hand in a broad arc, encompassing the piles of jumbled metal all over the field, "was their ship. I ordered it dismantled so no one else with the same ideas could use it, and also so that we could use the parts. We can always do with more metal, especially when it's already been refined and alloyed for us."

Kirk looked over the piles of scrap metal, and he had a sudden vision of the *Enterprise* itself ending up the same way some day, piles of anonymous junk from an old and decommissioned vessel, that left him shaken. Quickly, he said, "The message from Trellisane—did they say what their problem was?"

Kepac's face turned grim. "Not really. However, they did refer to the Klingons. That's another reason I wanted to tell it to you in private. The message was weak and garbled and that's virtually all we could understand. Let's get back to my office and I'll have a recording of it played for you."

Chapter Two

The prisoners were three Earthmen, two very humanoid women from Nactern, and a four-sex marital grouping, physically bonded for life, from Onctiliis. Since the latter creature was amorphous in shape, an almost featureless ball about a meter in diameter, only the Earthmen and the Nactern women were manacled. Had Kirk never heard of the surprising strength and agility of the innocuous-looking Onctiliian group creature, he might have made the mistake of taking the least care with that prisoner. As it was, he knew better, and he didn't need Lerak Kepac's warning to order the *Enterprise* Security men to take special care with it. "They move without warning," the governor told Kirk. "And fast. One of our colonists was crushed by the thing before we learned to keep weapons trained on them at all times."

When the group had all been beamed up to the *Enterprise*, Kirk personally saw the nine prisoners safely installed in detention cells in the Security section before he returned to the bridge. McCoy had preceded him and, on Kirk's orders, was telling Spock what he had seen of the prisoners. Kirk sat in the raised commanding officer's chair in the center of the bridge and allowed himself a full five seconds of blank-minded relaxation. Then he said, "Navigator, I want a course for Trellisane. Helmsman, take us out of orbit as soon as the course is available. Warp 3 all the way."

Behind him, Spock and McCoy exchanged a look of surprise. McCoy made as if to speak from the raised platform where he had been talking to Spock, but the Vulcan first officer raised his hand in a peremptory gesture, left the platform, and walked casually over to a position behind the captain's chair, and only then spoke to Kirk, quietly, in a voice no one else on the bridge could hear. "Captain, I must remind you of the high priority Star Fleet Command has placed on our putting these prisoners under its control as soon as possible. This incident has great political ramifications."

Without turning around, and suppressing a smile, Kirk said, "I'm well aware of the political aspect, Mister Spock. However, the prisoners will have to keep for a while. I'll want you, Scotty, and McCoy in the conference room in an hour, and I'll tell you why we're going to Trellisane. Tell them."

Kirk got up and walked over to the communication officer's console. "Lieutenant Uhura," he said quietly, "send the following message to Star Fleet Command, scrambled. 'The following message was received at Trefolg from Trellisane. I am proceeding to Trellisane immediately to investigate. James T. Kirk, commanding, *U.S.S. Enterprise.*' Then follow with this." He handed over a small disk, a copy of the recorded message he had heard on Trefolg. He waited until the message had been sent and acknowledged from the other end, then retrieved the disk from Uhura and turned to leave the bridge.

"Captain," Uhura said in surprise, "aren't you expecting a reply?"

When Spock had referred to the incident's political ramifications, he had been as accurate as always. Kirk chuckled at the thought of the command echelon at Star Fleet Headquarters trying to balance the two explosive issues, the prisoners and the mention of a Klingon threat. "Eventually, Lieutenant." He left the bridge, thinking that by the time a reply arrived, he would have reached Trellisane and would possibly be too involved to be ordered to leave until the problem was solved.

The first officer, the chief medical officer, and the chief engineer were gathered in the conference room, waiting for the captain, who had not yet arrived. Star Fleet law, Star Fleet custom, and the particular interplay of personalities aboard the *Enterprise* had given these men a triple role to play with which they were not always comfortable. Each had charge of major functions involved in running the ship. Together, they formed something of a council of advisers to the captain. And each, in a different way, was James Kirk's personal friend. Against these duties, they had to balance their duty to Star Fleet, the Federation, and, most immediately, the hundreds of men and women on the *Enterprise* whose well-being depended upon them. If they agreed that the captain's behavior was due to mental illness, or that his command abilities had been impaired significantly by physical illness, or even that he was simply behaving contrary to the best interests of Star Fleet, the Federation, and the personnel of the ship—for example, for reasons of personal gain or advancement—then it was their duty to remove him from command and to place one of their number in command. Personal friendship and admiration inevitably clouded such judgments, and every one of them would give James Kirk every benefit of the doubt before suggesting such a drastic step. Still, Kirk knew he would make their lives easier if he briefed them immediately on his reasons for ignoring his orders and heading for Trellisane. His reasons, in fact, had been the subject of their discussion in the conference room while they waited for him.

"Mr. Scott," the first officer was saying, his calm, Vulcan face and even tone giving no hint of the tension he felt, "you seem to be unaware of the dangerous nature of the prisoners we have onboard. I'm sure the captain feels he has good reasons for proceeding to Trellisane immediately, but I also believe he is mistaken in not being more concerned with getting these prisoners to a safer place of detention, such as a starbase, or preferably Star Fleet Headquarters."

Scott snorted. "That bunch? Three spindly men, two women, and a ball of flesh. The *Enterprise* can handle them!"

"Appearances and your prejudices have deceived you, Mr. Scott. One of the Earthmen is Hander Morl, a brilliant organizer and rabble rouser. The other two are his bodyguards, and although you may consider them unprepossessing, they are both members of the ancient cult of Assassins, able to kill quickly with every weapon known to civilization or with no weapons at all. The two women are the products of a warrior rite on Nactern and in their own way just as dangerous as the two Assassins. And as for the ball of flesh—well, perhaps you'd best tell Mr. Scott what you saw on Trefolg, Doctor."

Scott turned to McCoy, who grimaced and said, "One of the most smashed-up human bodies I've ever seen. Squashed flat by that creature, the Onctiliian. And apparently it happened before the victim could even get his weapon out."

Scott's confidence had been noticeably shaken. "It looks so harmless," he muttered. "Almost like a pet."

"I would advise against stroking it," the First Officer remarked mildly, causing the other two to wonder if this was a rare case of Vulcan humor or a sober caution. "The Onctiliian consists of four separate creatures, but they are physically bonded for life. The Onctiliians are unique in the known Galaxy for their, ah, tetrasexual method of reproduction. However, the bonding serves

15

other purposes, as well. In particular, it creates beings who have four distinct personalities residing in them but are still roughly four times as strong and as fast as a single Onctiliian. The four can pool their intelligence to a degree when necessary, and they will react with utmost speed and violence to any threat to their physical integrity. If one of them dies, all die: once the bonding has been completed, there is no way back for them. Instead of making the group creature more cautious, more timid, as one might expect it to, the opposite seems to be the case. An Onctiliian group creature attacks any threat ferociously, but also very intelligently, hoping to disarm and destroy it before the Onctiliian itself comes to harm."

Scott shook his head, his expression one of distress. "Och," was all he said.

Kirk strode briskly into the room. "I'm sure you're right, Mr. Scott. First, I want all of you to listen to this." He drew from his pocket the small recording disk he had earlier given to Uhura and slid it into the small combination console on the center of the table. "Computer, play that back."

A voice filled the room. "To the United Federation of Planets, or any associated planet or colony that receives this broadcast. Greetings from Trellisane." The weakness of the voice indicated a speaker of advanced age, but the four men had the impression of a mind that was both strong and wise. They listened quietly, intrigued. "We are not accustomed to asking for help from others, and we are reluctant to do so now. However, we believe the threat to Trellisane is great, and the source of that threat will surely be of concern to you as well." At that moment, the voice faded away, replaced by a wash of subspace noise, whispers of dying stars and interstellar dust. Through it, they caught only fragments. ". . . growing power of Sealon . . . definite signs of Klingon influence . . . military vessel to help us . . ." After that, the message faded entirely, and only the ancient noises of space could be heard.

"That's enough, computer," Kirk said softly, and the noise died away. The room was silent. Kirk broke the silence. "Both Governor Kepac on Trefolg and I interpret that to mean that Trellisane is being threatened by their neighboring world, Sealon, and that the Klingons are behind it. That makes it of concern to the Federation. Furthermore, I consider the last fragment to mean that they request help from us in the form of a military vessel. The *Enterprise* is the only ship in a position to get to Trellisane in a reasonable amount of time."

Scott, concerned more by the technical aspect of the problem than anything else, asked the room at large, "Now, why didn't they keep repeating the message? That way, we might have eventually put together the whole thing."

"Perhaps they couldn't," McCoy said. "Jim, we can't do anything against the Klingons anyway, because of the Organian Treaty."

"It's not a matter of us against the Klingons, Bones. The whole situation is a very complicated one. Computer, display a map of the Romulan and Klingon Empires and the Federation exploration territory, designating the stellar system containing Trellisane. Look at this, gentlemen."

The wall before them was converted into the requested map, a map whose general outlines were as familiar to all of them as the corridors of the *Enterprise*. In the center of the map, which represented the Galaxy as if it were two-dimensional and they were looking down at it from above, was the circular area which constituted the treaty exploration territory given over to the United Federation of Planets. Far smaller, to Galactic east along the Perseus and Orion arms of the Galaxy, stretched the Romulan Empire, separated from the Federation territory by the shaded Neutral Zone. To the west, its boundaries denoted as indefinite, lay the Klingon Empire, larger than the Romulan territory but still smaller than the Federation, at least as far as the computer knew. The barrier between Klingon Empire and Federation was titled ORGANIAN TREATY ZONE. Kirk, for one, was oppressed as always by what the map made so obvious: the Federation was considerably larger than either of its two great antagonists now, but the only direction available to it for expansion was toward the Galaxy's center, a most unpromising direction, while both the Romulans and the Klingons could swell outward along the Galaxy's spiral arms until they met a power great enough to stop them. The Irapina might do that job with the Romulans, and before too many more centuries had passed, but there was no reason to think the Klingons would be limited at all. They might yet become the Galaxy's dominant power, and despite the Organians' prediction of a future alliance between Klingon Empire and Federation, Kirk was often pessimistic about the Federation's distant future.

Near the limits of the map, in a fuzzy area where the Romulan Neutral Zone, the Organian Treaty Zone, and the Federation Treaty Exploration Territory itself all merged, a tiny red light winked. "That," Kirk said, pointing at the light, "is the location of Trellisane. To say it's in a sensitive region would be an understatement. Trellisane has had occasional contacts with the Federation, primarily in the form of trading vessels from some of the outpost colonies along the Romulan Neutral Zone. They have also independently invented subspace radio and have had some spotty communication with Federation planets that way. Currently, the conditions are very unfavorable for subspace communication in that sector, and so no one has heard much from them for a few years. When last heard from, the Trellisanians were on the verge of exploring their own stellar system in ships driven by impulse engines.

Obviously, they are a gifted and inventive people, and the Federation would be glad to have them as soon as they qualify for membership. Also obviously, both the Romulans and the Klingons could be expected to object violently to that as an intrusion by the Federation into the treaty zones. Trading vessels are one thing, permitted by both treaties, but actual membership would be another."

"I'd like to see either of them stop us," Scotty said hotly. "If those people want to join us, of their own free will, no one can object."

"There is a complication," Kirk said mildly. "Mr. Spock, perhaps you'd like to explain the complication."

"Certainly, Captain. I believe, Mr. Scott, that there is another habitable world in the same stellar system as Trellisane. That is Sealon, to which the subspace message we just heard must have been referring. Sealon is further from the primary it shares with Trellisane, larger, cooler, and almost covered with water. The only known intelligent species on Sealon is an aquatic mammal, large, strong, and primitive. It is also quite barbaric and warlike. These animals have reached a stage of aquaculture of plants and animals along the world's few continental shelves, and have rude settlements in the shallow water—the beginnings of city states. There is a perpetual string of raids and small wars between these settlements, with much killing and plundering of the lower animals and plants the Sealons cultivate. I would say that you humans should find them far more compatible than you will the Trellisanians, who are said to be quite civilized and peaceful."

"Thank you, Mr. Spock," Kirk said hastily. "Any questions?"

"Just one," McCoy drawled. "Why do we need any computers on this ship when we have Spock?"

Spock opened his mouth for a quick reply, but Kirk spoke first, firmly and loudly. "To return to the matter at hand, *gentlemen*. If the message from Trellisane does indeed mean that the Klingons have visited Sealon and are arming the natives, or in any way trying to absorb that world and extend themselves in that direction, then we cannot remain aloof. Even if the Sealons are willing recruits, the expansion of the Klingon Empire into that star system threatens Trellisane, and we can't simply ignore that."

"It's the same thing all over again, then, isn't it?" McCoy burst out. "War again, ships lost, men crippled. We're just starting all over again. What the Organians tried to do to stop us—it doesn't matter, after all. We and the Klingons are finding a way around it."

"Bones, perhaps the Organians shouldn't have interfered," Kirk said gently. "If we and the Klingons do manage to come to terms some day, we'll do it on our own accord, and not because some outside force has made us do it. Right now, however, we have an immediate problem. I'm sure you wouldn't want us to let them conquer a peaceful, progressive people like the Trellisanians while we sat back and did nothing to stop them. I'm also sure Star Fleet Command will agree with me, when it finally gets around to making up its mind and sending me new orders."

McCoy sighed and slumped down in his chair. "Yeah, I suppose so. I'm sorry, Jim. It's just that I'd like, some day, to be able to look forward to a career of just fixing up minor injuries from shipboard accidents. Phaser burns and explosion wounds are so messy and unpleasant."

Kirk said to the room at large, "I'd like to think that what I'm doing will help make your wish come true sooner."

Chapter Three

Captain's Log: Stardate 7526.4

The *Enterprise* is in orbit about Trellisane. I have
spoken to Veedron, a member of one of Trellisane's many *gemots,* or ruling councils. Veedron's
is the voice in the message recorded on Trefolg.
He has promised to explain to me how their
system of government works, but his more immediate concern is the threat to Trellisane. I am
scheduled to beam down and speak to him about
it shortly.

Kirk hesitated for only a moment before adding,
"Since Star Fleet Command has not yet responded to
my message, I am proceeding on my own initiative in
this matter."

Perhaps such malice was ill-advised. Upper-echelon
resentment could kill a career quickly, no matter how
illustrious an officer's accomplishments. There would
still be time, however, before the contents of the log
were transferred to Star Fleet central records, for Kirk
to "correct" its contents.

He thumbed the communicator button on the arm of
his chair and said briskly, "Security Section Chief."

A moment later, the reply came. "Kinitz here, Captain." The calm, confident voice, radiating strength and efficiency, gave a true image of the man.

"What's the status of the prisoners from Trefolg, Mr. Kinitz?"

"All secure, Captain." A faint tone of puzzlement. Prisoners under Kinitz's control were always well secured, so why was Kirk bothering him?

"Thank you, Mr. Kinitz. Carry on."

At that moment, Sulu said, "Captain! Vessel approaching from dead ahead. Collision course."

Kirk's response was swift and virtually automatic. "Full power to screens. Lieutenant Uhura?"

There was a short pause while Uhura tried to contact the other ship. "No response on any frequency, Captain."

The other ship loomed on the screen that covered the wall facing Kirk. While Uhura had tried and failed to contact it, the ship had grown from a negligible, moving dot among the stars to an onrushing juggernaut that filled the screen, blanking out both the stars and the curve of Trellisane's horizon. There was no time for evasive maneuvers. Instinctively, Kirk clutched the arms of his chair. The design of the attacker was familiar: a Klingon warship, even though its hull lacked any markings.

The attacking ship veered off at the last moment, and sighs of relief filled the *Enterprise*'s bridge. "Mr. Sulu, arm main phaser banks. Spock. Klingons, trying to warn us off?"

"So it would appear, Captain," the Vulcan said thoughtfully, "although there are subtle differences in the design that suggest otherwise. If it *is* a Klingon ship—"

"Captain!" Sulu broke in. "Here it comes again! Should I fire?"

"Calmly, Mr. Sulu. Only if I give the word." Kirk had completed for himself Spock's unfinished sentence:

"If it *is* a Klingon ship, then they cannot truly attack without violating the Organian Treaty." But then, Kirk thought, there's never an Organian around when you need one. He watched the screen tensely. Once again the other ship grew from a small point to a screen-filling monster, and once again it veered off in time.

When the ship appeared ahead of the *Enterprise* for the third time, instinct told Kirk that this would be it. The Federation ship had not changed course, had given no evidence that it intended to leave Trellisane. If the attacker's purpose had been to frighten the *Enterprise* into leaving, then they must know by now that they hadn't succeeded. They still hadn't responded to Uhura's attempts to communicate. They were almost surely planning to attack on this pass.

Instinct was right. This time the attacker did not rush headlong at the *Enterprise*. Instead, it established orbital station keeping near the limits of phaser range, did nothing for a moment, and then fired its phasers at the *Enterprise*. The jolt to the ship was less than Kirk had expected. Malfunction in the enemy's weapon? A warning shot? That was the enemy commander's problem, not his. "Mr. Sulu, fire main phaser banks."

"Aye, Captain."

Kirk prepared himself mentally for a long and hard-fought battle. He could only hope that no civilian areas on the planet below were damaged by badly aimed shots. The twin beams of the main phasers shot across the screen and met at the distant object that was their attacker. A flash of light, a soundless explosion, and the other ship had disappeared. There was a stunned silence on the bridge and a bad taste in Kirk's mouth. The enemy had been unprepared; the fight had scarcely been fair.

Spock, his eyes covered by the face-fitting molding of the science officer's readout device, broke the silence. "Captain, the explosion byproducts indicate that was definitely not a Klingon ship. The alloys were not the

Klingon fleet's standard, and there is a very high proportion of water vapor."

"Water vapor, Mr. Spock?"

"Ice now, Captain, but I presume it was water that was vaporized when the ship blew up."

"Uhura, get me Veedron on Trellisane immediately. Mr. Spock, conclusions?"

"Tentatively, Captain, that the ship was built on Sealon and crewed by Sealons. In that case, Klingon interference in this system has progressed even further than you had feared."

Kirk nodded. "Yes. I was hoping you'd have concluded something else. Uhura?"

"I have him, sir."

The picture on the large screen—stars in the upper half and the planet's rim in the lower, the lighted half slipping away as the *Enterprise* moved over the terminator—was replaced by an image of an older man, dressed in colorful robes. The background indicated a richly furnished and hung room. His face, however, showed signs of great fatigue and worry. "Captain Kirk. I am Veedron. Thank the gods you survived that attack!"

"Veedron, surely you could have warned us it was coming?" Kirk made no attempt to hide his anger.

Veedron shook his head. "No, Captain. We keep watch on objects in orbit, but nothing further than that. I will explain the reasons when I see you." The picture faded away.

Kirk drummed his fingers on his chair arm. Then he contacted the Security chief again. "Mr. Kinitz, I'll want a Security detail in the landing party, after all. Three men. Send them to the transporter room right away." After Kinitz had acknowledged, Kirk spoke into the communicator again. "Medical Section. Bones, you're going down to Trellisane with me. Meet me in the transporter room." He swiveled his chair around and stood up. "Mr. Spock, you will come, too."

Spock raised his eyebrows in silent surprise. Kirk smiled. "I would say it's time to show the flag and impress the natives. I get the impression that something has scared the Trellisanians witless, and I'd like our visit to have a real impact on their morale."

"And their allegiances, Captain?" Spock asked.

"That, too. Mr. Sulu, you have the con."

When they were alone in the elevator, Spock said to him, "Captain, the idea of fighting a war against the Klingons *via* proxies has disturbing ramifications."

"I know that, Mr. Spock. But so does letting the Klingons take over this system by force without any action on our part. Other uncommitted worlds will be paying attention to what happens here, and so will the Romulans. Nothing exists in a vacuum, Mr. Spock, not even in space."

Spock's expression was pained, but he said nothing.

Chapter Four

Veedron was taller than Kirk—almost as tall as Spock —but he managed to give the opposite impression through frequent bowing and repeated apologies. After suffering through this for some minutes, Kirk could stand it no more, and he said firmly, "I assure you, Veedron, we don't blame your people for that attack. I wish you had been able to warn us, but I accept your word that you couldn't. Now, I'd like to get to the reason for your distress call."

"The attack!" Veedron said. "That *is* our problem. We are under frequent attack, almost constant. We never know when it will come, or what they will bombard. The ship you destroyed was probably on its way to attack us. They noticed you, and you seemed a more tempting target."

"'They'?" Kirk asked.

"Sealons, of course."

"But, sir," Spock objected, "according to our most recent information, the Sealons are still far too primitive to have achieved space flight. Even with Klingon help, it will take them a generation to reach that level, and we know the Klingons have not been interested in this system for that long."

Veedron sighed. "It wasn't the Klingons who helped

the Sealons along: it was we Trellisanians, to our infinite regret. One moment, gentlemen." They had been standing in the room from which Veedron had spoken during his earlier contact with Kirk; the landing party had beamed down to that spot. Except for the communicator on one wall and the handsome tapestries on the walls, the room was empty. The furniture Kirk had noticed in the background during his conversation with Veedron from the ship was missing. Now Veedron clapped his hands once, and servants entered from doorways concealed by the tapestries. They carried small tables, chairs, and trays with food and drink. The room was converted to a low-key banquet hall within minutes. Veedron seemed transformed at the same time—from the obsequious, frightened man who had greeted them upon their arrival to the dominant figure in the room. Kirk could more easily believe now that this was indeed the man who had sent the message he had heard on Trefolg; now the man more closely matched the impression the voice had given. "You see," Veedron said, smiling, "we can still be civilized and treat guests properly, no matter what the external problems might be. Let us put off discussion of Sealon, please, and eat and drink and talk of other things."

The time seemed interminable to Kirk, but experience had taught him to put on a good front for diplomatic purposes. He chafed at it, though, and wanted to get right to the point of their visit. Should he show his impatience, no doubt Veedron would classify him and his companions as barbarians. Too much depended upon making the right impression, so Kirk schooled his face to an expression of polite enjoyment and waited.

The food and drink were delicious, and the variety and quantity were both abundant. The cuts of meat, especially, were exotic and exquisite. Kirk could not detect on his companions' faces the same impatience he felt. At last, however, it was over, and, with a sigh of regret, Veedron assumed a more businesslike pose and returned to the main subject.

"Well over a generation ago, Captain, our ships made the first voyage to Sealon. By Sealon standards, that would be two generations ago. As you probably know, they are a warlike people, killing or subjugating each other without compunction." He shuddered at the thought. "The first Trellisanian expedition was almost wiped out when it tried to make contact with the Sealons. The few who survived were able to return and tell us their horror story." He took a reflective sip of wine from an ornate goblet. "After a lengthy discussion between the leaders of the *gemots*, we decided that the Sealons needed to be helped along the path of civilization and peacefulness. It was clear to us that their belligerence was due to their undeveloped state. With our help, they could outgrow all of that." An expression of deep pain crossed his face. "We lost many more of our citizens before we could establish contact with them. Their hostility and cruelty were virtually mindless. Those we sent were killed before they could communicate our intentions. We persisted, though, seeing it as our duty to our lesser developed brothers, who are after all children of the same star." He paused, staring off into space.

"Obviously, then, you managed to make contact with them eventually," Kirk prompted.

"Oh, yes, of course. We persisted, trying different locations on their planet. In time, we came across one Sealon city state whose leader was a being of some vision, one who ordered his underlings to let our people live until they could learn his language and explain their mission. When they had done so, he welcomed them and all the help we wanted to give him. They're quick learners, the Sealons. They passed through the stages of civilization much faster than our own ancestors did." He said this with some bitterness. "Before long, this leader, Pongol, had extended his domination over much of his world. Sealon has few land masses, and those are small. Pongol chose one such land area as his technical center. Under his successor, Matabele, we led them to the stage of space flight and subspace radio. On the land mass chosen by Pongol, they now have an impressive technically and industrially oriented city, and their own space port. We had expected them to use both their radio and their ships to increase their cultural and commercial contacts with us, to our mutual benefit. Alas, that was not to be." Once again, he became lost in his thoughts.

Kirk, growing increasingly impatient at Veedron's circuitous, drawn-out style of storytelling, prompted him again. "I suppose their warlike nature remained."

"Yes." As if he wanted to get through the next part of his explanation as quickly as possible, Veedron spoke much more briskly than before. "Yes, they hadn't changed, after all. Once they had learned what they could from us, they killed all the Trellisanians within their territory and cut off contact with us. Unknown to us, they had already used their subspace radio to speak to the Klingons, and now they invited the Klingons in. Under Klingon tutelage, they learned to arm their space ships, and then they undertook a war against us."

"They also modified their ships along Klingon lines," Spock remarked.

"Yes. In general, they found the Klingons far more to their taste than they did us."

Kirk snorted. "They might change their minds when they learn the Klingons' true intentions."

Veedron's hand fluttered, dismissing that argument. "I doubt if they have any delusions about that, even now. The Sealons, and Matabele in particular, are a supremely confident species, possibly with some justification. I'm sure they plan to absorb all they can from the Klingons, just as they did earlier from us, and then turn against them. No doubt the Klingons will react more vigorously to that than we did."

"How did you react?" Kirk asked the question, but he thought he could anticipate the answer.

"We retreated. Quite simply, we turned inward completely. We were filled with guilt as much as with fear. There was an extraordinary council of all the *gemots* at which the decision was made to abandon all space flight and concentrate on our remaining domestic problems. We had done evil on Sealon; we had also put ourselves in danger from them. We hoped that, with our space ships gone, they would choose to ignore us and go their own way."

Kirk shook his head. "Of course that didn't happen. That path never works."

Veedron said, "I was one of the few who opposed that path of action. Fortunately, I was able to gain a compromise: we retained our subspace radio installations. The Sealons did not ignore us. They soon began to attack us here, on our own world. At first, we couldn't decide what to do. We still feared going back into space ourselves, and we were afraid we would antagonize them even more if we tried to. Then the Klingons approached us with an offer. If we would join their empire willingly, they would protect us from the Sealons."

McCoy blurted out, "Don't trust them, for God's sake!"

"Calmly, Bones," Kirk said. "He's right, of course. You can't trust them. They would never try to take over by open force. They know that would bring us in in a hurry. However, if they can honestly say that you invited them, as the Sealons already have, then we have no excuse to intervene. That was when you tried to contact us?"

Veedron nodded. "We agreed we had no choice but to reopen contact with the outside. As you have already noticed, we have no defenses. We no longer have any detection devices beyond orbital sensors. Trellisane also has a large ratio of water to land area—about two to one—with very large continental shelves. The Klingons implied they would gladly equip the Sealons to make landings on those shelves so that they could begin to colonize Trellisane. We would be left with nothing when it was all over, not even our lives."

"If we agree to defend you, I hope you realize fully what sort of Galactic politics you'll be getting involved in."

Veedron was about to answer when Kirk's communicator bleeped. He took it from his belt quickly and flipped it open. "Kirk here."

Sulu's voice. "Captain, we're under attack again. This time, there're three of them." His voice was interrupted by loud noises and the gabble of voices in the background.

"Sulu! What's happening up there?" The men from the *Enterprise* sat tensely, mentally projecting themselves back onto the ship and trying to imagine what was happening onboard. "Sulu!"

"Sorry, Captain. It was a bit worse this time than last. They have screens, so we couldn't get at them so easily. We've taken one of them out of action, but the other two are still making passes. There's been some damage. We can't beam you up while this is going on. I'll get back to you as soon—" There was a loud crash, followed by silence. Kirk looked around the room helplessly, imagining the worst.

Endless minutes passed. Veedron went quietly to the wall communicator and spoke in low tones to the central office which coordinated the orbital sensors, but they could add nothing significant to what Sulu had already said.

The communicator bleeped again. "Captain Kirk?" A smooth voice, well modulated, unhurried.

"Yes! Who is this? Where's Sulu?"

"Sulu is well, Captain, for now. This is Hander Morl. I am now in command of your ship, and I have some unfinished business to attend to, business your treasonous friends on Trefolg interrupted. I thought I would do you the courtesy of informing you before the ship departed from orbit. One commander to another. Console yourself with this thought: your ship will be sacrificed to the good of the Federation, and you will survive its destruction. You may lose your commission because of this, but once the war with the Romulans gets well underway, there should be ample opportunity for an able man like you to work your way back up the command ladder again. Good-bye, Captain." The communicator clicked off, and there was no further response, despite Kirk's repeated attempts at contact.

"My ship," Kirk muttered disbelievingly. "They've got my ship." Beside that fact, Trellisane and all its troubles faded into insignificance.

Chapter Five

Sulu had been overconfident. When the three attackers were first detected, he ordered only half power to the ship's defensive screens, convinced that this enemy's weapons would be no more potent than the first attacker's. These three came in with their own screens up and they were therefore not as vulnerable to the *Enterprise*'s phasers as Sulu expected them to be. Nonetheless, the *Enterprise*'s first shot put one of them out of action, even though it didn't destroy it.

The remaining two fired simultaneously and at the same point on the *Enterprise*. The *Enterprise*'s defense computer responded quickly, decreasing screen power elsewhere in order to reinforce the point under fire, doing the best it could under the constraint Sulu's order of half power had placed upon it. It was not quite quick enough. During the picosecond delay before the computer issued its command and the few nanoseconds following that before the command was implemented and screen power could build up, the Sealons' beams sliced through the weak screens. What struck the hull was much diminished in strength by its passage through the screen, but it was strong enough.

The beam hit the main hull and ruptured several layers of the metallic outer skin. This was where the

Security section was located. The impact sent Security personnel reeling against furniture and walls. Kinitz, the section's chief, was off duty and was resting in his quarters; the concussion threw him from his bunk. He landed on the floor in a half-crouch, snapping awake and reacting instinctively at the first shock. For a few moments, the lights in his cabin went off. The Sealons' phaser beams had cut through the main power supply to the Security section; by an almost impossible coincidence, the shock waves from the exploding outer skin had so degraded the section's self-contained emergency power unit that seconds passed before the lights in Kinitz's cabin came flickeringly and weakly to life again. In that dim half-light, Kinitz waited impatiently for the door of his cabin to open slowly. As soon as he could squeeze through the opening, he ran down the hallway. His worry approached frenzy: uppermost in his imagination was the image of the guardian beams of the detention cell doorways cutting off for those few vital seconds. Uncharacteristically, Kinitz made a mistake. He neglected to use the communication module in his cabin to alert his men to the possibility of an escape.

Kinitz's worst fears were justified. The beams had cut off for a few seconds, and one of Hander Morl's bodyguards leaped instantly through the doorway and into the corridor beyond. The other Assassin, in an adjacent cell and not quite as quick-witted as his colleague, didn't move until he saw the other man already in the hallway. By then, the beams had come back on, although weakly, and the second Assassin was flung back against his cell's far wall, unconscious from the blast to his nervous system.

Hander Morl himself and the two Nactern women watched all of this with no reaction. But the Onctiliian group-creature, estimating the weakness of the beams from the dimness of the flash they made when the second Assassin hit them, gauged its own chances differently. It rolled back to the far wall of its cell and then threw itself forward at the doorway. There was a flash and the smell of burned flesh, but the creature's momentum carried it through. It rolled to a stop in the corridor, weak and exhausted. One of its four components, the one most exposed to the beams, had been knocked unconscious. The other three Onctiliians quickly reorganized their mental union, reassigning life functions so that the unconscious member was properly cared for; the resulting intelligence, reduced though it was, was still greater than a man's.

Recovered thus far, the Onctiliian took note of its surroundings again. It saw the Assassin vanish around the curve of the corridor, and it saw nothing by the doors of the detention cells that would enable it to turn off the beams and release the others, so it rolled down the corridor in the direction opposite to that taken by the Assassin.

The Assassin found the control panel only a short distance further on. A young Security guard had been seated at a small desk before it, reading a book while keeping a desultory watch on the corridor, but the impact seconds earlier had thrown him from his chair. He had hit his head on the floor and was only now climbing groggily to his feet. He never quite made it. The Assassin reached him before he could get his feet under him or his hand on his weapon or the alarm button. With the guard lying dead next to his desk, the Assassin studied the labels on the control panels briefly, then pushed a series of buttons. He picked up the dead guard's phaser, looked at it for a moment in contempt, then shrugged, put the weapon in his belt, and headed back toward the cells.

Meanwhile, the Onctiliian, still feeling somewhat disoriented, came across three Security men in the corridor and stopped in momentary confusion. The men were rubbing their bruised shoulders and elbows and discussing their shaking-up in loud voices. Although a Condition Red had been announced and the men knew the *Enterprise* was under attack, they had no specific defensive duties, and they were griping loudly to dispel their feelings of tension and helplessness. One of them happened to glance down the corridor and noticed the Onctiliian sitting quietly in the middle of it, as if it were listening to their complaints. "Look," the Security man said softly, nudging his neighbor, "what's that?"

The other man looked over his shoulder, then shouted, "Jesus, it's one of the prisoners!" He grabbed his phaser from his belt and fired at the alien.

Without conscious thought, the Onctiliian had stopped with its nonfunctioning component facing the humans. The phaser was set on "stun," always the standard setting for men under Kirk's command, but the comatose Onctiliian caught the full force of the blast. Because of the smaller size of the individual Onctiliian body and the greater complexity of its nervous system, what would stun a man could be a dangerous shock even to a healthy Onctiliian; weakened as it already was, the unconscious component died.

The shock of its death tore through the three surviving Onctiliians. A high-pitched, three-voice scream echoed down the corridor—an astonishingly sweet sound, a Siren song. The cry momentarily paralyzed the three security men. The Onctiliian, enraged and bewildered, flashed down the hallway, a blur the men could scarcely see. It left two of the men as long red smears along the walls and the third one with a crushed side. Deranged, the Onctiliian rolled down the corridor, randomly killing or crippling some of those it encountered and ignoring others.

Spock had been somewhat mistaken in his information about Onctiliians. In this, he could be excused, since little was known about them in the Galaxy at large. While it was true that the death of one of the four physically bonded individuals had doomed the group-creature as a whole to death, that death would not come as rapidly as Spock had implied. The first effect had been madness: physically powerful and mentally potent as the three-part creature still was, its sanity could not survive the sudden loss of one-fourth of what had been itself. It was not that which doomed it, however, but rather the poisons from the dead member even now spreading through the bodies of the other three. Even if it had stayed sane, it could not have divested itself of the corpse. The attachment between the four was profound, thorough, and eternal. The dissolution of a dead Onctiliian was rapid, and its effect on the others—the effect of the proteins, digestive acids, and other biochemicals its death had released into their bloodstreams—was inevitable and irreversible, but it could take hours or even days to finally kill them.

Kinitz appeared before it. He fell into a crouch, his phaser pointing at the Onctiliian, but it suddenly swerved to one side and through an open archway. Kinitz hurried forward. The archway was the entrance to a cargo and service ramp that led downwards in a spiral path to lower levels, and by the time Kinitz got to the opening, the Onctiliian had disappeared. He hesitated for a moment, afraid of the damage the creature might cause below, but he knew the greater danger lay ahead of him: it was far more important that he find Hander Morl, the leader of the prisoners, and take him captive again if he had escaped.

Further along the corridor, Kinitz came across bodies and parts of bodies. He also found the survivors. He had no time to talk to the well or help the injured. He ran faster. At last he came across a tableau that brought him to a quick halt, his phaser coming out. Hander Morl stood in the center of the corridor, tapping his foot impatiently, while his bodyguard bent over the other Assassin, lying on the floor, and slapped his face hard and regularly, trying to bring him back to consciousness. The man on the floor stirred and groaned and tried to raise his arm to protect his face.

"All right," Hander Morl snapped. "That's good enough. Get him to his feet and let's get moving."

"Moving back into your cells," Kinitz said calmly. Morl and the Assassin spun around, and the bodyguard poised himself. "Don't," Kinitz said, grinning at him. "I know what you are, but this is faster." The Assassin relaxed again.

Kinitz had made his second, and last, major mistake. Worried first about Hander Morl, the prisoners' leader, and then more immediately about the deadly Assassin bodyguard, he had dismissed as unimportant the Nactern warrior women. They had both pressed themselves up against the corridor walls when they'd heard his footsteps, and they were hidden from his sight by the bulge of a turboelevator shaft. "Back into the detention cells," Kinitz repeated, stepping forward, his phaser held unwaveringly on the two men before him. They backed away as he moved forward, drawing him past the two women's hiding place.

He saw the movement from the corner of his eye, but before he could react, a boot slammed into his wrist, knocking the phaser flying, and something hit him in the small of the back with a crushing, stunning blow. Kinitz's legs folded under him, and even as he fell, he was hit on the side of the neck.

Kinitz lay helpless on the corridor floor, his vision fading. He heard a man laugh, and he could see one of the Nactern warriors' boots in front of his face. At the end, he realized it had been the women, not the Assassin, who had broken his back and neck. He willed his lungs to breathe, but the will that could cow the strong men who worked in the Security section could not control his own body, and Kinitz's consciousness and life slipped away.

Hander Morl wasted no time on triumph. "Pick up

his phaser and follow me," he snapped. He himself had the phaser the Assassin had brought back with him. The Assassin and one of the Nactern women half-carrying the other bodyguard between them, the group hurried after Morl. The other Nactern warrior caught up with him. "What about the Onctiliian?" she said.

Morl shrugged. "If he shows up, he can rejoin us. I never entirely trusted him, anyway." From the plans he had studied while designing his substitute starship, Hander Morl knew enough about the *Enterprise*'s layout to be able to find the turboelevator that would take them to the bridge. By the time they all piled into it, the second bodyguard had recovered sufficiently to stand unassisted, and they were all armed with phasers picked up along the way from the dead left behind by the Onctiliian. The wounded they passed, they finished off.

The elevator hummed and lurched along silently. The group of United Expansionists within it waited stolidly, weapons at the ready. When the doors swished open, showing them the bridge spread out before them, they moved quickly.

Sulu was in the command chair, talking into the communicator. "I'll get back to you," he was saying. Morl raised his phaser, aimed at Sulu, and pressed the firing stud. Sulu jerked as the beam hit him, then collapsed against one arm of the chair. Until that moment, the attention of everyone on the bridge had been concentrated on the huge viewing screen at the front of the room, where the two Sealon ships could still be seen maneuvering for another pass at the *Enterprise*. Now they found themselves staring into the muzzles of the phasers held by Hander Morl and his followers, and there was nothing any of them could do.

Hander Morl stepped jauntily over to the command chair, rolled Sulu out of it onto the floor, and sat down. "All right, everyone," he announced. "I'm in command here. Get back to work and get us out of here. I want this ship headed for the nearest point in the Romulan Neutral Zone as soon as possible and at the highest speed available. You," he said to Uhura, who was still staring at him in openmouthed amazement, "you're the communications officer, right? Where's your captain?"

"Uh, he's down on the surface of Trellisane," Uhura replied, her response to a question from the command chair virtually automatic. A moment later, she cursed herself for having said anything.

Morl laughed. "Wonderful! Get me in touch with him, right now." Uhura turned grudgingly to her equipment, and Morl spoke to Chekov, who had turned around to stare at him. "If your captain's down there," Morl asked him, nudging Sulu with his toe, "then who's this?"

"That," Chekov said, anger thickening his accent, "is Mr. Sulu, and if you've hurt him, all your weapons won't help you."

Hander Morl smiled. "A commendable sentiment, but the welfare of the Federation should count for more to you than the well-being of your friend." He gestured one of his bodyguards over. "Now this man, you see, will wake your friend up and then see to it that Sulu dies in grotesque agony while you watch, unless you follow the orders I gave a moment ago."

Chekov looked at the tall, heavily muscled Assassin and at the man's utterly cold expression; then he gritted his teeth and turned to his console to plot the course Morl had requested.

"I have the captain," Uhura said, her voice sullen.

"Captain Kirk?" Morl said into the chair's communicator.

"Yes! Who is this? Where's Sulu?"

"Sulu is well, Captain, for now." As Morl spoke, the Sealon ships made two more passes. After the first attack, Sulu had corrected his mistake and had ordered full power to the ship's defensive screens. The Sealons' phaser beams now caused only a slight tremor to run through the hull of the *Enterprise,* and there was no damage. The personnel on the bridge didn't notice even that, for their attention was riveted on the drama happening near them and on Morl's taunting words to their captain. "Good-bye, Captain," he said at last and signaled Uhura to break the contact.

Chekov had laid in the course and alerted the engine room. He felt there must be some way he could relay the appropriate orders to Scotty, some cryptic phrase he could use, that would alert the chief engineer to the situation on the bridge. His mind seemed frozen, though, and he could only speak and act mechanically, as if the man in the command chair were Captain Kirk himself and the orders Chekov was following were routine. He thought of laying in a course to the nearest starbase instead of to the Neutral Zone, but something in Hander Morl's intelligent face told him that the man would know if he did so, and Sulu's life would then be forfeit. Well, Pavel Andreievich, he told himself, it will take a couple of days to reach the Neutral Zone. There are only a few of them, against more than 400 of us. That should be time to think of something. What would Captain Kirk do in this situation?

But while Chekov searched for alternatives, the *Enterprise* responded to its engines, left orbit under impulse drive, and then headed from the Trellisane system at warp speed, leaving the puzzled Sealons behind.

Chapter Six

Whatever small encouragement Veedron had drawn from the arrival of the Federation officers on Trellisane had instantly deserted him once he realized that, with the loss of their ship, they were now as weak and ineffectual as he was. "I'd better request another council of the *gemots*," he said gloomily. "We must decide on a new course."

Kirk had been staring into space, not lost in thought, but helpless and hopeless, stunned by the loss of his ship. He had never felt quite so abandoned, so lost, his very foundation removed. McCoy leaned toward him and said softly, "Jim. *Captain* Kirk!"

Kirk shook himself. "Thank you, Bones. Veedron, you said you had abandoned space flight. What about your ships?"

"We destroyed them, I'm afraid. Those few that were left, that is, after the initial Sealon attacks. None of our ships had weapons or defenses, you see."

"Of course not," Kirk said bitterly.

"Captain," Spock said, "the Trellisanians' ships could not have been used to pursue the *Enterprise*, in any case, since they lacked warp drive technology."

"That wasn't quite what I had in mind, Mr. Spock."

A tremor shook the room and there was a muffled booming noise from overhead.

"The Sealons," Veedron said, collapsing still further. "Now that your ship is gone, they've gone back to their original mission of bombarding us." He shook his head. "I cannot bear to think of all the deaths."

"You surely have medical emergency teams, don't you?" McCoy asked.

Veedron looked bewildered. "We have our hospitals, of course, and physicians, and emergency services for individual medical problems. Much of that becomes inoperative during these attacks, however. Ambulance pilots cannot fly during bombardments. Power supplies to hospitals are disrupted. We pride ourselves on how well we handle individual medical emergencies, but the system breaks down in these conditions. Even if we could get all the wounded to hospitals, the staffs could not handle such numbers."

"Good Lord, man," McCoy said angrily, "don't you ever have natural disasters or wars?"

Veedron's distaste was evident. "None of us lives where there is a chance of natural disaster. All of our cities are restricted to the safest zones. And we have not had a . . . war . . . since the most ancient times. Surely you don't have wars in the Federation now?" His voice rose. "Surely such a civilization as yours can avoid natural disasters?"

McCoy's mouth quirked into a wry smile. "Let's just say that a starship medical officer learns to handle large numbers of injuries under less than ideal conditions." He turned to Kirk. "Jim, maybe I could help these people organize teams, medical strike forces. That all right with you?"

"Yes, Bones, of course. Veedron?"

"Do you mean you could help us deal with the injured?" the Trellisanian said. Hope appeared on his face for the first time. "Come with me, Doctor! We'll give you whatever support you request." He jumped to his feet and led McCoy from the room.

After they had left, Kirk said quietly, "Well, Mr. Spock, I see now even more clearly what we're up against here. The Trellisanians have an enviable reputation for ingenuity and ambition, but it seems they avoid adversity rather than meeting it face-to-face."

"Yes, Captain. I noted that Veedron offered Dr. McCoy whatever support he feels he needs, rather than asking him just to help them with his broader knowledge. They expect him to take the lead, to provide all the initiative, because their dilemma is unprecedented and frightening. Captain, you expressed a desire a few minutes ago to use a Trellisanian ship in some manner, but not to pursue the *Enterprise.* May I ask what your plans are?"

Kirk hesitated for a moment. "I don't think I should tell you too much, Mr. Spock, for your own sake. Even if I manage to bring all of this to a successful conclusion, it won't look too good on my record. We're in this situation because of my insistence on heading for Trellisane with the prisoners still on board. If I don't pull off what I have in mind, then my career is certainly over." He laughed, but it was a bitter sound. "You don't attain command of a starship in Star Fleet without making some enemies along the way, and they don't go away. They stay around, waiting for their chance. I may have just given it to them. You're still clean, and I want to keep you that way. You made your objections known to me when I first decided to come here before delivering the prisoners; that was your duty. If you know what I plan next and help me despite knowing, and if I fail in the end, then your own career might be ruined along with mine. I don't want to be responsible for that, too."

Spock nodded. "Sufficiently logical, Captain. Tell me only what you wish."

"Good. What I want is to get in touch with the

Klingon naval commander on Sealon. However, I want to be able to speak to him from a position of strength. Therefore, I don't want the Trellisanians to contact the Klingons and surrender abjectly. I wouldn't want them to do that, in any case, but without some sort of meaningful Federation protection, I expect that's just what they're going to end up doing."

Spock raised his eyebrows. "There is a limit to how much interference we can risk, Captain. We cannot violate either the Prime Directive or the Organian Peace Treaty."

"I'll keep all that in mind, Mr. Spock, but the alternative may be a full-fledged war between the Federation and the Romulan Empire. The choice of risks is a clear one for me."

Those below had no hint of it at first, but this attack on Trellisane was to be different from all those which had preceded it. The bombardment tapered off, but the Sealon ships didn't depart from orbit and return to Sealon as the Trellisanians had learned to expect. Instead, the two which had not been disabled by the *Enterprise* raised the already high inclinations of their orbits until both ships were in virtually polar orbits.

The high inclinations of the three ships' initial orbits had been chosen to allow them to pass over the major industrial, scientific, and urban targets in both the northern and southern hemispheres. To the Trellisanians manning the radar stations and other orbital sensor installations on the planetary surface, nervously watching their screens and readouts, the purpose of the change to polar orbits seemed obscure. But to Kirk and Spock, who were with Veedron when he was told of the orbit changes, a reason suggested itself immediately.

Veedron had been conducting them on a depressing tour of a rubble-filled site—the aftermath of a recent Sealon attack. The damage was cleared away and the buildings replaced as soon as the Trellisanians could manage, but destruction always takes less time than construction, and the Sealon attacks had been so frequent and closely spaced that the Trellisanians could not hope to keep up. The site Kirk and Spock were being shown when the message was delivered had been the last remaining subspace transceiver on Trellisane. The Sealons must have intercepted the Trellisanian appeal for Federation aid, for it was immediately after that initial transmission, the recording of which Kirk had heard on Trefolg, that Sealon ships had appeared at Trellisane for another attack; the transceiver had been their primary target.

In the middle of explaining all of this to the two Star Fleet officers, Veedron stiffened and his eyes took on a glazed look. The three of them were standing on the edge of the crater that had been the subspace radio emplacement. What had once been parkland stretching away from the emplacement in all directions was now sterile, blasted earth, with here and there a jumbled pile of dead tree trunks. Veedron's bright, ankle-length robes stood out sharply against this dreary background, making him look like an exotic bird creature from elsewhere who didn't belong here. He stared abstractedly into space, ignoring his two guests.

"Spock," Kirk said softly to the Vulcan. "Some kind of seizure?"

Spock looked up from the handful of soil he was examining and glanced at Veedron's face. "I would say, Captain, that Veedron is in communication with someone."

"Telepathic contact, you mean?"

Spock frowned. "I've received no hints of that since our arrival, no impression of telepathic communication."

Veedron sighed suddenly and shook himself. "Captain Kirk. Mr. Spock. I must apologize for my rudeness. I've just been told that two of the Sealon vessels still in orbit about Trellisane have shifted into polar orbits rather than leaving for home. This has not happened before, and I fear it cannot be a good sign, although I am at a loss to explain their actions."

"Only two?" Kirk asked. "Three attacked the *Enterprise.*"

"The third was crippled by your ship. It remains in its original orbit, but its altitude is low. Drag is significant, and its orbit is decaying."

Spock said, "Sir, a polar orbit suggests a detailed mapping mission."

"Perhaps you're right," Veedron said dispiritedly. "Perhaps they're choosing targets for future bombardments."

"Or," said Kirk, "sites for a landing. The beginning of their invasion."

Veedron's reaction to this suggestion was a mixture of amazement and horror. "Invasion! We thought we had much more time! Please excuse me. I must seek seclusion and summon another council of the *gemots*. I fear this will tip the scale in favor of an immediate appeal to the Klingons."

As Veedron hurried off, Kirk said angrily, "Councils! Discussions! That seems to be their response to everything. There seems to be no one here, no individual, with the authority to act quickly in the case of a crisis."

"I would surmise, Captain, that Veedron and this world's other leaders or council members are linked electronically, by means of some sort of brain implant. That would explain both the manner in which he received that message and his current desire for seclusion. My inability to detect any form of telepathic communion supports my belief. If the ruling elite can all communicate instantly with each other, no matter where they are, their deliberations might be speedier and more efficient than one would at first think."

"Not efficient or vigorous enough to suit me. I can't let them invite the Klingons in. That would take away what little bargaining power I might have, and you know what would happen to this world under Klingon domination."

"I don't see what we can do to stop them."

"Perhaps not much by ourselves, but there must be *some*one on this planet with the guts and the will to fight back! We're going to find them, whoever they are."

Chapter Seven

Hander Morl did not delude himself that he and his four remaining followers were a match for the more than 400 trained personnel of the *Enterprise*. If he exercised sufficient care, there should be no confrontation: outside the bridge, no one would know that anything out of the ordinary had happened.

On a long trip, he knew, he could never have hoped to pull it off. There would have had to be relief crews for the bridge. Those off duty would have had to be guarded, which would have necessitated splitting his own tiny group up into two or three pieces. Food would have become necessary, eventually, and he could not imagine how he would have handled that. And it would have been inevitable that someone from elsewhere in the ship—Engineering, perhaps, or Medical—would have needed to talk to the officer in charge of the bridge. As it was, though, the trip should take no more than a day and a half, according to Morl's estimate, and he would simply keep the bridge sealed to outsiders, with his own two Assassins guarding the turboelevator doors rather than the usual two Security guards, and keep the present crew on the bridge for the duration. Once the *Enterprise* entered the Romulan Neutral

Zone and was destroyed, his purpose would be accomplished and he would no longer have to worry about these petty details.

Petty as the details were, though, Hander Morl was forced to admit to himself that they held a surprising appeal for him. It was as much the emphasis on order, duty, and obedience preached by the United Expansion Party as its philosophy concerning the destiny of the Federation to grow to dominate the Galaxy that had attracted Hander Morl to it. He believed in the Federation's duty and destiny to expand and conquer, but he also believed in an individual citizen doing his duty even to the point of personal sacrifice. That, of course, was why he and his followers were willing to die on this mission, and why he was angry at the knowledge that the crew of the *Enterprise* would probably not be willing, if he gave them the choice, to do the same. Personal death was a high price to pay, but it was a small price in exchange for forcing a war of conquest upon the reluctant weaklings who ran the Federation. It was not impossible that the crisis would bring down the government and that the war against the Romulans, when it finally came about, would be conducted under the control of the United Expansion Party itself.

Morl had always derived great pleasure from submitting himself to the will of the UEP leadership. He obeyed his orders without question, just as he expected his own subordinates to obey his orders. He had hoped that some day he would be invited to join the leadership himself, but if that never happened he would still school himself to be content. This mission was his idea; party leadership had jumped at the idea and immediately placed Morl himself in command of the mission. Now he would never rise higher in the UEP: he had known from the start that there would be no returning from this mission. He accepted that, too. To be chosen for this task was honor enough, even greater honor than commanding some section or brigade of the party. In the future, school children of the Galaxy-spanning Federation of Planets would learn of his exploit, would study his life. He would be one of the greatest martyr-figures in Federation history. Still, sitting at this hub of power, feeling the lines of command stretching throughout this magnificent space vessel, binding more than 400 people into an obedient whole, and converging in the raised chair on the bridge where he, Hander Morl, sat—this was a pleasure and an honor, too, even if he had not attained the position legitimately. No, he told himself quickly. Put that thought from you. My goals confer all the legitimacy I need. If the Federation were being run as it should, someone like me would already be sitting here.

The *Enterprise* was still in an alert status. Hander Morl had heard the alert sounded *via* the wall speakers outside his cell. So far, despite the ship's departure from the scene of the battle, the alert had not been canceled. He had no idea if a day and a half was a long time for an alert to be maintained or not—if that might make someone outside the bridge suspicious—but maintaining it had at least one advantage. As long as the alert was in force, everyone on the ship would be too worried about what was going on invisibly outside the hull to concern themselves with the lack of crew changes on the bridge. Or so Hander Morl hoped. And there was a good excuse for maintaining the alert status: the escape of the prisoners from the Security section!

He motioned one of the Nactern women over and pointed at Sulu, who was still lying on the floor where Morl had dumped him but was stirring and groaning. "Get him on his feet. Quickly." If there were any announcements to be made, Morl didn't want alarm spread by a stranger's voice on the ship's speakers.

The warrior woman picked Sulu up easily and held

him on his feet. His head lolled on his chest and his legs were rubber. "I meant, wake him up!" Morl said impatiently.

She shook Sulu and slapped him hard a couple of times, and at last he could stand by himself. He held his head in his hands and tried to make his stomach settle itself. The phaser had been set on "strong stun," and Sulu's head felt as if it would fall to the deck in pieces if he let go. As his vision cleared, he looked around the bridge and saw the armed intruders, their weapons moving slowly back and forth to discourage all thoughts of heroism. His mind was still fuzzy from the phaser bolt, and he had no idea who Hander Morl and the others were, but it was clear enough to him that they were in at least temporary command of the *Enterprise*.

"Sulu!" Morl snapped. "Come over here. I want you to make an announcement."

His knees still weak but growing stronger, Sulu obeyed. Following Morl's orders, he thumbed a button on the command chair arm and announced the continuation of the Red Alert. "The escaped prisoners could be anywhere on the ship by now," he said, half listening to the amplified sound of his voice echoing faintly through the walls of the bridge. "Red Alert will be maintained until all have been recaptured. They are to be considered extremely dangerous. Alert procedures will be followed until further notice. Bridge out."

Morl nodded. This one at least knew his duty and did it. "Return to your normal post on the bridge, Sulu." His tone came close to being kind.

In the Medical section, Nurse Christine Chapel muttered in annoyance. With McCoy presumably still down on Trellisane, and his other assistants off tending to the wounded in the Security section, where the damage seemed to have been confined, she was virtually alone in Medical. Normally, she could have handled that with no difficulty, equipped as she was both by training and temperament to keep everything running properly. Quite a few badly mangled Security personnel had been brought to her, however, and the automated medical equipment was getting badly overloaded. She needed more than two hands to stay on top of things. For that matter, long exposure to Dr. McCoy had prejudiced her in favor of the human touch and against the mechanical, so that she felt morally bound to tend to each patient herself, no matter what the machine knitting the patient back together said about the patient's progress. The continuation of the Red Alert, just announced over the speakers, meant that she could not requisition any kind of help: everyone who could fulfill a duty had one assigned during such alerts, and no one, of those who might be of use to her, would be available to come down to Medical and place himself under her orders. Dr. Goro, who would normally have taken charge of Medical in McCoy's absence, had called in only minutes earlier to tell Chapel that he was staying in the Security section because of what he called "the carnage here" and had no idea when he'd be able to get back to Medical section.

It was while she was sitting by the bedside of a young woman from Security, whose pallor seemed to indicate to Chapel that she was not doing at all as well as the life-support equipment claimed, that she heard a thin, high-pitched noise behind her that she knew didn't belong here. She turned quickly, then gasped in astonishment.

At the far end of the room, jammed up against the wall as though using it for support, was a creature unlike any she had seen before. It was a roughly spherical thing, perhaps a meter in diameter, its color somewhere between pink and brown. She had not been present when the prisoners had been brought aboard, and she had heard nothing about them since then. Knowing nothing at all about Onctiliis and its four-sex group creatures, she had no idea what this thing was.

Her first reaction to it, nonetheless, was fear. Its high-pitched, sweet-sounding cry continued, and it cut through her, fascinating and repelling her at the same time.

Then Chapel saw that one side of the being, turned almost away from her, was oozing fluids; and as she watched it, the Onctiliian began to lose its spherical shape and to slump down, flattening more and more against the floor until it had no recognizable shape. "Why, you poor thing!" Chapel said. "You're badly hurt." It was due more to a feeling she received from the creature, this conclusion of hers, than to analysis. After all, she knew of shapeless creatures whose slumping down to the floor was no reflection on their state of health; similarly, she had seen beings who oozed fluids as part of their normal functioning. Somehow, she felt a communication of some kind come across the room to her, an impression that all of the Onctiliian's defensive ferocity had left it and that it was pleading for help.

Chapel's instincts and training asserted themselves, and she got up and went quickly over to the Onctiliian, filled with the desire to help this latest patient. Essential as speed so often was in medical emergencies, she had long ago learned not to seem to be attacking a frightened, wounded alien. She kneeled slowly before it and gently placed her hand on it, near the place the fluids were oozing from. The high-pitched cry softened and stopped at last. She could almost feel the dying creature relax under her comforting touch.

Earlier that day, rushing about trying to take care of the needs of all the wounded and nearly dead being brought into Medical, Chapel had cut her hand badly, stripping off a few square centimeters of skin and flesh on her palm. Her own wound had been minor, in her opinion, compared to those of the patients being brought in, and if it hadn't been for the way it had interfered with her ability to function properly, she would have ignored it. As it was, she had dressed it hastily and forgotten about it. Now, losing consciousness at last, the Onctiliian twitched, and Chapel momentarily lost her balance and fell forward. Her hand slid across the smooth, wet skin and plunged into the body of the dead Onctiliian.

Disorganization, putrefaction—these followed quickly upon death for an Onctiliian. Indeed, it was largely this rapidity of decay that doomed the other three Onctiliians in a bonding to death, for a longer grace period would give them time to expel the dead member and find a replacement. Chapel's hand sank into the flesh up to her wrist, and she cried out in horror.

A fragment of bone within the dead creature had caught on the dressing as Chapel fell forward, and now the dressing and the scab beneath it were torn off together. Her hand sank through the almost liquid body of the dead member and came to rest at last against the junction, the boundary, with one of the living three, her flayed palm resting full length against the communication nexus and the fluid interchange.

Chapel toppled over onto her side, her eyes glazing. She felt herself falling and falling, and then held firmly, both comforted and trapped. She opened her mouth to cry out again, this time in renewed fear rather than horror, but the sound that came from her, echoed by the group-creature, was that high-pitched, utterly inhuman Onctiliian cry of pain and bewilderment. A new communication was established, a new joining had begun, stranger and more exciting than any that had gone before.

Had nothing out of the ordinary happened on the bridge—neither the takeover by Hander Morl and his men nor the attack by the Sealon ships which had made the takeover possible—the bridge crew would all have been relieved within a couple of hours after Morl's phaser had knocked Sulu out. As it was, those on the bridge had already spent two normal shifts trapped in that relatively small place, and they were all dreaming, not so much of freedom from the phasers pointed at them, as of hot meals, hot showers, and warm bunks with warm companions in them. It was very surprising, Ensign Chekov told himself, that he should keep thinking about and missing all those little pleasures and comforts of daily life, rather than worrying about the deeper issues: here the *Enterprise* was in the hands of a gang of criminal madmen, headed for the Romulan Neutral Zone, Chekov and his comrades apparently unable to do anything to retake the ship, and all Chekov could think of was his growling belly and his drooping eyelids. Ah, Pavel Andreievich, he thought, it's just that your backside is killing you from sitting here for so long.

Chekov reached both arms up and stretched slowly and thoroughly. It didn't do anything for his aching buttocks or cramped legs, but it helped relieve the tension in his shoulders and back. He turned his head from side to side, wincing at the throbbing of a growing headache. For the first time, he noticed the Nactern warrior standing near his chair and gazing at the huge front screen in fascination. Well, well, he asked himself, what's this?

Her expression was one he had seen before, one he had worn on his own face for days on end when he was first assigned to the bridge. It was virtually impossible not to be captivated by the star field as seen on the forward screens of a ship in warp drive. Color shifts and relativistic distortions were compensated for automatically by the computer controlling the screen display, so that what showed on the screen was what Spock liked to call "a Newtonian analogue" of the scene a suited crewman on the forward hull would see, but in a way the result was even more entrancing. Dead ahead, in the center of the screen, the stars seemed motionless, as of course they were. Toward the edges of the screen, however, the ship's incredible velocity showed in the way the multicolored sparks crawled radially away from the center. Some stars were close enough to the ship's path to seem to move independently of the others, crawling past in front of them with an increasing speed that could induce vertigo in the inexperienced viewer.

Never mind that the Galaxy was stable, moving only with astronomically slow majesty, and that what the screen showed was merely an artifact of the ship's motion and the computer's ingenuity: still, the unwary viewer could easily find himself lost in the illusion that *he* was the only fixed point in a twisting, flowing Universe, where constellations formed and dissolved as he watched, and the Galaxy rushed past on all sides, hurrying off to some unimaginable destiny behind him. Despite the simulations he had been shown beforehand and the warning he had received, Chekov had fallen prey to that illusion during his first days on the job, and it had kept him bewildered for days. He had experienced the phenomenon then himself, and he had seen it happen often enough to other newcomers, but he had scarcely expected to see it happen to one of these singleminded fanatics, and especially not to this cold and rather masculine woman. Use whatever the gods give you, he told himself.

Chekov leaned toward the woman and said, "It's a dangerous illusion."

She shook herself at the sound of his voice and said in a bewildered voice, "What?"

"I said that it's a dangerous illusion. You can lose yourself in it and become nonfunctional." He explained quickly how the display on the screen was produced and how it differed from what they would be seeing if it weren't for the computer's processing of the image. She smiled at him in a friendly way. Chekov relaxed and began both to put more effort into it and to enjoy himself. Among the things he had always admired most about James Kirk was the captain's ability to switch from terrifying martinet to charming and tactful gentleman.

Behind Chekov, Hander Morl watched and smiled cynically. Let the young fool try, thinking he's so clever, Morl thought. It will keep him occupied. Destiny is only hours away.

Chapter Eight

What arrived to take up a circum-Trellisane orbit only hours after Veedron's departure was quite different from anything Sealon the Trellisanians had seen before. It was huge, dwarfing the Sealon attack ships they were growing accustomed to. By all their sensors' indications, it was virtually amorphous, utterly lacking that Klingon-inspired bird-of-prey configuration they so feared. This strange, blobby thing circling their planet at low altitude and low inclination—it was an anticlimax, it was almost a laughable object. The leaders of Trellisane, Veedron and the other heads of the many *gemots,* felt hope revive at last: perhaps the Sealons had come to their senses and would cease their aggression!

The crippled Sealon attack craft, left behind in a low orbit when its two companions had raised their altitudes and shifted to polar orbits, had long since succumbed to drag, spiraling ever lower until it deorbited and screamed down through the atmosphere, a brilliant fireball, its remains impacting on a large, uninhabited island near the equator. Ever highly moral, ever softhearted, the Trellisanians had rushed one of McCoy's new emergency medical teams to the spot to care for any survivors. Of course there were none. Now the huge new arrival, in just as low an orbit, began to break up. The Trellisanians watched the destruction—hinting at a loss of life far greater than the earlier disaster—with utmost horror. How could they watch such a tragedy and stay unmoved? They summoned the temerity to broadcast a message to the huge craft: "Raise your orbit! Can we help you in any way?" There was no reply from the Sealon vessel.

At last the Trellisanian observers realized that the great ship's breakup was no accident. The pieces that separated from the main bulk were all of roughly the same size, and they detached themselves at regular intervals, deorbited under apparent control, and splashed gently into Trellisane's oceans. Soon all that was left in orbit was a giant framework, the skeleton of the monster that had arrived in orbit, with one end bulging out to form the housing for impulse engines. This skeleton left orbit and departed upon the long coast back to Sealon. The invasion was underway.

Kirk and Spock had managed to obtain transportation back to Veedron's headquarters building, which was in fact the administrative headquarters only of the Protocol Binders *gemot,* the *gemot* of which Veedron was head. With the advent of the Sealon crisis and because of Veedron's acknowledged eminence among the council of *gemot* leaders, the building had become the closest thing Trellisane had to a governmental center. Observation of the orbital sensors had been transferred here from the headquarters of the Orbit Traffic Controllers *gemot* on another continent, and it was here that Kirk and Spock watched helplessly while the Sealons' invasion force deorbited and vanished beneath the surface of the seas, unhindered by Trellisanian vessels in space, in the air, or on the seas.

"They used to call them 'beachheads,'" Kirk said, forcing a smile. "We'll have to coin a new word." For just a moment, he feared the Vulcan would take him seriously and try to provide the new word.

Veedron was not there when they arrived. Nor did he show up as the hours passed and the evidence accumulated that the Sealons were establishing themselves in Trellisane's oceans with an air of permanence and an attitude of aggression. Spock remained impassive, but Kirk fumed at his own impotence. Reports came in a steady stream, detailing the Sealons' cool destruction of what little remained of the Trellisanians' ability to resist them. First, ships already at sea began to disappear. From the few eyewitness reports from aircraft, whose pilots told of seeing explosions dotting the surface of the oceans, it was clear that Trellisanian shipping would be destroyed immediately upon detection. Shortly afterwards, contact began to be lost with the aircraft themselves, those that were over the open sea. The Sealons had not only come prepared to stay; they had also brought with them weapons that could eliminate any craft flying over their new domain. All too obviously, it would only be a short time before they attacked the Trellisanians on land. Even those few Trellisanians with the courage to resist would by then be too weakened to do anything, for the sea was their main source of food, and that was to be denied to them.

A subtler kind of attack soon manifested itself. Kirk, raging inwardly but knowing how futile any outward display of anger would be, left the operations center, where Spock remained to watch with detached, clinical interest, and roamed the halls of the great building. Kirk felt that he needed to do something physical, anything, even if that was no more than aimless wandering. And he came across Veedron, curled into a ball on the floor up against one wall of a corridor, still in his colorful robes, like a tropical bird that had been crushed by some winged predator and then cast aside.

Veedron was still alive, but he didn't respond when Kirk spoke his name and grasped his shoulders. His eyes were open, but they stared unseeing at Kirk, with no hint of either recognition or intelligence in them.

Kirk cursed and looked quickly up and down the hallway. No one was in sight. He pulled his communicator from his belt and flipped it open. "Bones! Where are you?"

There was a few seconds' delay, and then McCoy's voice spoke from the communicator in miniature. "McCoy here. Jim? What's wrong?"

"That's what I want you to tell me, damn it." He told the doctor where he was. "Get one of your teams here as soon as you can. Something's wrong with Veedron." Silently he added, *Veedron's not much but he seems to be the best we've got, and I want him preserved.*

"Veedron. Well, in that case, Jim, I'll come myself. Sit tight."

Kirk bit off an angry response, saying instead only, "Kirk out," and flipping his communicator closed. *Won't do to take my feelings out on one of the two good men on the planet. Restraint is the word. Sit tight, he says!*

Subjectively, it seemed forever before McCoy arrived, but Kirk checked his timepiece half unconsciously and realized that the time was very short. He was mightily impressed by the speed of McCoy's response; it indicated to him what a fine job the doctor had done of organizing an emergency response system under these very trying conditions. All he said, however, was, "Can you bring him out of it?"

McCoy was kneeling beside the curled-up Trellisanian leader in the hallway. Now he straightened, drew a hypospray from his equipment pack and pondered its settings for a moment. "Probably." He fiddled with the device for a moment, then shook his head. "And to think my instructors used to spend so much time worrying about what's ethical and what isn't. I'd like to see one of them deal with a war." He leaned forward again and applied the spray to Veedron's arm. There was a faint *whoosh*. "No physical damage that I could detect," McCoy said, meanwhile preoccupied with another tricorder examination of his patient. "Some sort of mental shock, I'd guess. What I just gave him should shock him out of it, at least temporarily."

As if at a signal, Veedron groaned and relaxed from his fetal curl. He muttered something, scarcely understandable. He cleared his throat and tried again. "Captain Kirk? Is that you?"

Kirk kneeled beside him. "Here, sir. I found you on the floor, unconscious." He chose not to mention the wide-open, empty eyes nor the position of Veedron's body.

"Yes, yes. Thank you for helping." Veedron struggled to his feet and stood swaying, the two Star Fleet officers supporting him on both sides. "I was standing here, in the hallway, engaged in a worldwide meeting of *gemot* delegates." He looked around as if in wonder, still dazed. "There was no one here," he explained, his voice almost that of a trusting child whom someone had injured, "and I thought it would be a good place to be while communicating with the others. Suddenly, there was a blast of sound, of noise, *in my head!* The others went away, disappeared. Not all of them, just those on other continents." He wailed in despair: "They're gone! I'll never talk to them again!" Tears streamed down his face and he pulled his arms from the supporting hands and fell to his knees, his shoulders heaving with his sobs.

McCoy took out his communicator and quickly called his Trellisanian helpers. "We'll keep him in bed and sedated until he can recover enough to take care of himself," he said in a low voice, as if he were speaking more to himself than to Kirk. "Damn it, I shouldn't have shocked him awake, after all. That trance may have been a natural Trellisanian defense mechanism against trauma. I hope I haven't done any permanent harm."

Kirk listened but didn't respond. "Worse and worse," he muttered. "Or perhaps not." He knelt down, close to Veedron. "Veedron!" he said sharply, but the Trellisanian was too deeply sunk in his sorrows to hear. "Veedron!" Louder this time, but still no response.

McCoy pulled him away, his face suffused with rage. "Damn it, Jim, leave him alone! We may already have done him irreparable harm."

Kirk ignored him and took out his communicator again. "Mr. Spock."

"Spock here, Captain."

How Kirk valued those calm and calm-inducing tones at such times as these! "Mr. Spock, do you have any indication that the Trellisanian leaders' communications with each other may have broken down, that their implanted communicators may no longer be operable?"

"One moment, Captain. I shall enquire." A minute of silence; two minutes. Then Spock's controlled voice again. "Indeed, Captain, the technicians monitoring those channels locally say they can no longer establish contact with their opposite numbers on the other continents. It would seem that the Sealons have instituted some type of blocking or jamming action to prevent such communication. I cannot guess whether or not they will be able to extend that jamming over the airspace of the continents themselves."

"It scarcely matters if they do, Mr. Spock," Kirk said thoughtfully. "Kirk out." Merely by cutting the *gemot* leaders on each continent off from those on all the other land masses, the Sealons had managed to paralyze the already ineffectual Trellisane governmental structure. The natives had managed little enough in their own defense before this; now they would be able to do nothing.

"Jim," McCoy said, "what was that about an implant?"

Kirk quickly explained Spock's surmise to him.

"Hmm. That's interesting." McCoy put his hand in

his pocket and fiddled with a centimeter-long cylindrical capsule he had put there only minutes earlier. He had recovered it from the brain of a dead servant, victim of a head injury in an earlier Sealon bombardment, whom he had been vainly trying to save. Kirk's communicator call had come just as McCoy was admitting defeat: another loss to his oldest adversary.

By now, the medical team called in by McCoy had arrived and were removing Veedron on a stretcher. McCoy went with them, casting an angry glance back at Kirk, who told himself, not for the first time, that McCoy's protective feelings toward his patients were just about the only thing that could ever cause the doctor to really seriously consider mutiny.

Kirk headed rapidly back toward the control center where Spock was still observing. As he walked, he pondered the latest change of conditions and tried to estimate the impact on his already bizarre circumstances. On the one hand, the dissolution of the local tenuous governmental system, based on long-distance meetings between the leaders of the various *gemots*—whatever in God's name those were, anyway—meant that the organization, the infrastructure, needed to organize some kind of resistance had effectively disappeared. On the other hand, though, Veedron himself had predicted that that government would have capitulated to Klingon; even if that hadn't happened, what Kirk had seen so far on Trellisane made him feel sure that the government would have been more of a hindrance than a help. Now that it was out of the way, he could feel unconstrained, could do whatever he felt was necessary. What that might be and how he could go about doing it, without the *Enterprise* being available, was another question, and perhaps a far more difficult one.

Kirk reentered the control center's main room and found Spock standing where he had left him, watching the technicians bustling about, on his face an expression as close to one of interest as Kirk could expect to see on a Vulcan. Kirk beckoned Spock to follow him out of the room. In the hallway outside, Kirk said, unknowingly echoing the thoughts of Ensign Chekov on the bridge of the *Enterprise,* now so far away, "It's very strange, Mr. Spock, but in the middle of this disaster I find myself most concerned with a sudden, overwhelming hunger. Do you know how we can get some food to fuel us for what comes next?"

"From observing Veedron, I would say it is simple enough, Captain. Follow me." Spock set off down the hallway, and Kirk, after a moment's hesitation, followed him. The First Officer led the way to a room that Kirk recognized as the one in which he had first met Veedron. That time seemed years ago now; indeed, he thought, the change in Trellisane's condition since that time is of such a magnitude that, in peace time, it would have taken years or even generations to come about. "And now, Captain, I believe we need only do this." The Vulcan clapped his hands sharply, once. However, nothing happened. "Curious," he murmured.

Kirk grunted. "Veedron must have a flair that you lack, Mr. Spock."

Calmly, unperturbed, as if hunger and frustration didn't exist, Spock said to his hungry and frustrated captain, "By the way, Captain, I took the liberty of questioning some of the technicians in the control center concerning these *gemots* and their method of government. A fascinating system. It seems that governments of the type we know never really evolved on Trellisane, and neither did a religious hierarchy. What took their place was a vast collection of professional organizations, each representing a profession or trade or craft, much like the guilds of medieval earth. Those guilds are what they call *gemots*. Each handles matters within its area of competence. Any matter not thus covered is overseen by cooperative councils of *gemot* representatives, such as the supreme council to which Veedron belongs."

Kirk nodded. "That would explain their reluctance to do anything out of the ordinary, to take drastic action at a time like this. Even on earth in the Middle Ages, the guilds that ran the towns in Europe were often a force for conservatism, for things as they were. They protected the *status quo* as a shield against the hostile outside world."

"Precisely, Captain. And since there is no equivalent of the medieval overlord to oppose the *gemots* and threaten their power on Trellisane, there is no impetus to change and advance for their own sake."

"Fascinating, indeed, Mr. Spock, but my most immediate concern is my growling belly. Perhaps if I try." Kirk clapped his hands sharply, trying to imitate Veedron's manner of superior self-assurance.

This time, there was some success. The hangings on one of the walls parted and a servant entered the room. He approached the two officers hesitantly and bowed quickly. "Sirs, you wish something?"

"Yes, indeed," Kirk told him. "We'd like some food, a meal."

Anger flickered on the servant's face for an instant, then disappeared. He bowed again. "Many are dead, sirs, or requisitioned to help in the rebuilding and rescuing, but I will try to find someone to prepare food for you. Forgive me for any delay."

The man's anger and his manner, which indicated that the anger was still there but held rigidly in check, hinted at something important, and Kirk momentarily forgot his hunger. "Just a moment. 'Requisitioned,' you said?"

The servant's eyes darted from side to side nervously and he licked his lips quickly. He knew these two were from somewhere other than Trellisane, but clearly he did not know how far he could trust them. "Yes, sir," he said at last, reluctantly, "I said that. The Man Healers *gemot* requisitioned some, but most of them were taken away by the Builders *gemot.* And of course the Food Provenders *gemot* has requisitioned, too."

"But what about your own *gemot?* Doesn't it object to its members being . . . requisitioned . . . this way?"

The servant laughed harshly. "Our *gemot!* You must be joking." He looked them over and decided they were serious. Kirk could almost see the man make up his mind to trust them. "We have no *gemot.* Didn't the illustrious Veedron explain that to you?"

Spock said, "Veedron explained nothing to us about this world's social or governmental system. We have found out some things on our own and deduced others."

The servant's anger had returned, and this time he made no attempt to conceal it. "Then you didn't find out or deduce enough. Those of us who serve and tend our masters—we have no *gemot,* and we never have had one. No one protects us, no one pleads our cases. The only time a *gemot* or its members notice us is when we do something wrong. Anyone can punish one of us, and there is no *gemot* to stand in the way."

"Fascinating, Captain. This class of helots was never mentioned to us before, nor do I remember seeing any word of it in the reports I reviewed on the way to Trellisane."

Kirk's face was grim. "No, Mr. Spock, and it's clear enough why not. These aren't servants: they're slaves. The Federation would not have approved, and any negotiations over Trellisane's admission to the Federation would have gone by the board until this system was reformed. Now listen, Spock, I don't want to hear anything from you about the Prime Directive. Clear?"

Spock gazed carefully in a neutral direction.

"Fine." Kirk turned back to the slave, who had listened with both evident interest and confusion. "If your world can be saved from the Sealons and the

Klingons, then it will be obliged to turn to the Federation of Planets for future protection; it will almost certainly petition for membership. That will be to your advantage."

The servant snorted. "Klingon, Sealon, Federation, or the ones we have now. One master is no better than any other."

"No, damn it! The Federation is no one's master. Each world that belongs to it is the equal of any other world. And every single Federation citizen is the equal, before the law, of any other citizen. Do you understand that? It doesn't matter how many arms and legs you have, or eyes, or what things used to be like on your world before it joined the Federation. To become a member, a world has to guarantee every single citizen legal equality, and it has to adhere to all Federation legal and social principles in that regard."

"Equal!" The servant's eyes shone. "Does that mean we'd have a *gemot* of our own?"

Kirk laughed. "A *gemot!* Better than that: you'd have the entire Federation government behind you whenever you needed it—the biggest *gemot* in the known universe!" Then he said, harshly, breaking through the man's sudden reverie, "But not if the Sealons and Klingons succeed here. If they take over, Trellisane will never join the Federation. It'll become part of the Klingon Empire instead, and then you'll find out that some masters can indeed be much worse than the ones you're used to. We're no longer able to protect you, because our ship has been taken from us. The *gemots* are virtually paralyzed, both because of this communications breakdown and because it seems to be in their nature to be paralyzed. It's up to you—you slaves. You're the only ones left who can save this world."

"And then," the slave whispered, "we'll join your Federation, and *we'll* be in charge!" He turned and ran from the room.

"Captain—" Spock said quietly.

Kirk held up his hand. "I know, Mr. Spock. But what other reaction could we have expected? At any rate, we've found the men we want, the ones I said must exist somewhere on this world: those with something to fight for and the guts to do it. Let's try to win this war first, and then we'll worry about reeducating them." He paused for a moment. "Funny. I've lost my appetite."

Chapter Nine

McCoy was puzzled more than he was disturbed. He had found the tiny capsules in the brains of all the slave corpses he had examined, but not yet in the brains of any other corpses. Of course, he had not yet happened to have access to casualties of the uppermost class—Veedron's class, the *gemot* leaders, and he knew from what Spock had told Kirk that that class had brain implants of some kind.

Very strange, he thought, that only the topmost and bottommost classes would have it. Assuming it's the same gadget in both cases. Communication for the rulers, Jim said. But what about the slaves? What's it *for*? So that they can be given orders? Why not just speak to them, for that? In fact, they do speak to them, to give them orders. I can't get anything out of the Trellisanians. They act so ignorant and innocent.

The next day, as McCoy and his Trellisanian assistants were having a working lunch together—truly excellent steaks, very uncommon for the apparently vegetarian Trellisanians—when one of the slaves who'd brought in the food and was now standing in the background against a wall suddenly slumped to the floor. McCoy rushed to his side, tricorder out. "Complete brain death," he muttered. "My God. What the Hell . . . ?" Only then did he notice that none of his assistants had stirred from his place. All were staring at him with puzzled expressions. One of them—Pellison, the best of the lot—said, "Sir, Dr. McCoy, it's only a *yegemot.*"

Only then did it occur to McCoy that injured slaves had never been brought to him for treatment. Those he had worked on, he had come across on his own, while exploring the sites of Sealon attacks.

Two slaves came into the room, their faces expressionless. They picked up their dead fellow silently and moved toward the door.

"Hey! Wait a minute!" But they ignored McCoy's yells and tramped silently through the doorway with their burden. "Who called those guys? How'd they know to come? Who called them?" He looked around angrily. He got no answer.

Pain. Searing pain, dull pain, throbbing pain.
One hurts. Why?
Kidneys. Cannot cope. Other organs too.
Kidneys? What are those?
Waste eliminators. Cannot cope. They will fail. One will die. Pain throughout, then death. Release one. *Release one!*
Release? Meaningless. *We* are one.
Release me! LET ME GO!
The shouted thought, and its freight of hatred and fear, shrieked along the communication network. The creature recoiled in horror of its own, and Chapel rolled free, to lie gasping on the floor, vomiting.

At last she regained enough strength to climb unsteadily to her feet and minister to herself. Christine Chapel, research biologist with respected credentials and impressive achievements, as she had been before personal matters had led her to join the *Enterprise* crew as a nurse: apart from those instincts that urged her to help the wounded being, she was driven by the under-standing that she faced a professional challenge as great as any in her previous career and far greater than any she had encountered on the *Enterprise*.

Still shaking, she injected herself with a metabolic booster and certain blocking agents. She had more than guesswork to go on. Dim but present were memories of a greater, clearer intellect, which she remembered as having been her own, and an intimate knowledge of alien biological processes and how they had meshed with hers. She knew what the alien fluids were and their dangers and rôles; and she knew of the mental dangers and rewards. What she had injected into herself should at least protect her body.

Thus fortified and forewarned, Chapel approached the slumping Onctiliian again. She steeled herself and placed her hand very deliberately on the darkening, oozing surface of the dead one. She paused there for a moment, took a deep breath and held it. Then, firmly, smoothly, and without haste, she forced her hand through the viscid flesh until it contacted the nexus.

I have returned. *I* am here.

Ensign Chekov picked himself up slowly from the deck of the *Enterprise* and put his hand gingerly over his right eye. The flesh around the eye was already swelling out, forcing the lid shut. "Why," he demanded through gritted teeth, "did you do that?"

The Nactern warrior glared back at him, her eyes level with his. "You're lucky you're still alive!" she hissed. "Don't try that again, or I'll forget we need you on the bridge."

A bad miscalculation, he told himself, trying to convince himself that he was calm and collected. Let's try the innocent approach. "Why, I don't understand," he said, his tone denoting hurt bewilderment. "I thought you wanted me to kiss you. Was I wrong?"

"Wrong!" She laughed, a harsh, barking sound, but

her posture relaxed. "You're a harmless fool, after all. No one kisses me but my mate, and even she doesn't when we're in battle status, like right now."

"She—" At last a bright light dawned for Chekov. The other warrior woman on the bridge, of course, he thought. That's not a mistake I've made very often before. Now, what would Captain Kirk do in a situation like *this?* "I'm sorry," he said, looking as contrite as his swollen-shut eye allowed. "I didn't realize, or I certainly wouldn't have tried anything. Look, let's just forget what happened and continue collecting the food." They were in a deserted recreation room near the bridge, collecting the meals they had ordered through the small wall dispenser. Hander Morl had decided to make this small concession to human needs, believing that letting the bridge crew have a meal would help keep them from causing him trouble. Chekov had instantly volunteered himself and the warrior woman to do the job; to the ensign's considerable surprise, Morl had first laughed heartily and then agreed without argument. Turning to the trays of food he had ignored during his unsuccessful attempt at starting a seduction, Chekov said, "These should be enough. We can probably handle them between us. Look, there's no reason for hostility now that I understand, is there? We *are* on the same side, supposedly."

Unexpectedly, the warrior smiled at him. "Hander keeps telling us we are, but I'm not so sure, from the way the rest of your crew behaves toward us and our mission."

"Perhaps the others don't see the issues as clearly as I do," Chekov suggested. He walked over to a nearby table and sat in one of the chairs propped up against it. "Come on. There's no rush. Why don't you explain to me just what you people are really trying to do? All I've heard so far is the captain's version, and I'm sure that's biased. *You* can tell me the truth."

With all the eagerness of the true believer sensing the

presence of a possible convert, she took a chair next to his and began an impassioned lecture. She started with a complete history of the United Expansion Party, and the minutes ticked away.

On the bridge, Hander Morl began to worry. He struggled to keep his feelings from showing on his face. What was keeping those two? He didn't dare send one of the Assassin bodyguards to find them, for that would leave him with only two accomplices to keep the bridge under control, and he feared that might not be enough, not with the obvious fraying of tempers as time passed without food or sleep. The *Enterprise* personnel were growing both more desperate and more frustrated, and simultaneously, he and his three subordinates were losing their edge from the accumulation of tension and fatigue.

If he did send someone, he thought, it would have to be one of the Assassins. The Nactern woman would be more motivated, but she would also be more likely to behave rashly if Chekov had somehow succeeded in his very obvious intention. Morl needed Chekov; he knew that. He *couldn't* have succeeded, could he? Not with a Nactern warrior woman! Morl realized he was chewing his fingernails nervously, and he quickly and angrily pulled his hand away from his mouth.

None of the surgical hoods could be adjusted so far that they would accomodate the Onctiliian. Chapel was reduced to working with small, portable equipment. The capabilities of the portable devices were limited at the best of times, compared with the full-scale devices she would have preferred to use, and this was not the best of times: she was working one-handed, operating the equipment with her left hand while her right, still buried deep within the group-creature's body, maintained her mental link with her pain-wracked patient.

Fluids were injected, blocking the action of the decay

agents released from the dead member's body. Chapel herself was hooked into her machines *via* a separate set of tubes and wires, and fluids pumped rapidly through these in response to her commands; even while the human and Onctiliian metabolisms were joined through her hand, they had to be fed, boosted, and controlled separately by the machines. She had no help in this, had had no time to call for it, and felt oddly furtive, even ashamed, about her intimate communion with the alien. But she had hope, hope that she would succeed after all.

The first priority was to save the lives of the three surviving Onctiliians. Normally, all would have been long dead. Perhaps it was the Earth-normal gravitation on the *Enterprise,* considerably less than that on Onctiliis, that had slowed the deterioration so far. Perhaps it was the political commitment of this particular individual to the United Expansion cause, for most Onctiliians, once they had become part of a group mating, became fairly apolitical. Whatever the reason, the three living members, while close to death, still lived.

Even so, their death would have been certain in time. They had an intimate knowledge of and contact with their own biology, the inner processes of their group body, that probably surpassed that of any other creature in the known Galaxy, but they had few means of affecting those processes under such extreme conditions as these. They might know what was happening inside themselves, but they could only watch it happen helplessly. With Christine Chapel's intervention, that had changed. The technology available to her and the training and professional experience in her background would not have been adequate equipment for the rescue, either, under normal circumstances. But added to that was her psychophysiological link with the Onctiliian: what they knew, she knew; what they felt, she felt. She had little doubt that, if she were not interrupted, if she were granted the time, she could save them. What she would do next, was rather more problematical.

The Nactern warrior broke off her lecture on the aims of the United Expansion Party suddenly and stood up. "Come!" she commanded. "Too much time has passed. We must gather the food and return to the bridge."

Chekov protested, "But there are a lot of things I still don't understand. For example—"

"Enough! Now I understand what you're trying to do. You're not interested in our cause at all. We've wasted enough time. Come!"

He stood too and sighed. "You're right. I'm not really on your side politically. It was just an excuse to try to spend some more time alone with you, that's all." He grimaced ruefully. Long ago, a girl he had known well had told Chekov that he reminded her of a little boy and that brought out the mothering instinct in her. Now he tried hard to look as little-boy as possible. "Everything is so grim when we're on the bridge. Down here, we can talk and try to forget that we're all going to die soon."

"I never let myself forget what's important," she said harshly, her tone all grim and filled with duty. But her expression softened. She patted Chekov on the shoulder. "Come, now. When it happens, when the Romulans destroy us, it will be quick and painless, and I will be near you. Come."

Chekov picked up the trays and went along obediently, trying to convince himself that he hadn't failed entirely. Think of it as an investment, he told himself. Nothing comes of it immediately, but in the long run, the return can be significant. I hope the long run isn't too long, though.

When they reached the bridge, Chekov watched the invaders' reactions carefully. Morl tried to act nonchalant, but his relief was obvious. The two Assassins paid no attention. The other Nactern warrior looked her comrade and Chekov over carefully, then set her jaw as if she sensed something she didn't care for and moved pointedly away from her returned mate.

Chekov distributed the food and then returned to his post at the Navigator's Console. Sulu turned to look at him with seeming casualness, but his eyes held a question. Minutely, Chekov shook his head: no luck. Sulu turned to the front again, his disappointed hopes hidden from their captors but not from Chekov. I tried, damn it, Chekov wanted to say. We'll just have to hope for something else.

Done: they would live. She didn't know it, but this was the first time in the history of the Onctiliian race that a group creature had survived the death of one of its members. Chapel had already earned herself a footnote in medical history, should she care to exploit her achievement. But what was to come would dwarf even what she had already done. She had already made the beginning; now she was to confirm the creation of a being that had never existed before.

Sure that her patient was stable, Chapel at last relaxed her mental concentration and gently withdrew her hand from the communication nexus. The dead member, she had already removed. Now she covered the exposed nexus with a dressing and told the creature to extrude flesh and skin to provide a permanent covering. Only when that had been accomplished, under her careful scrutiny, did Christine realize that she had given that last suggestion, maintained that communion, without any physical contact.

No, she reminded herself, there was still one channel of contact: the portable machine that was steadily measuring the prescribed fluids and drugs into her bloodstream and the system of the Onctiliian. There was no more need for that, however, and she carefully detached it from herself. Still the communion persisted.

It was not so strong as before. She no longer felt her identity threatened by it. Or was it just that she had learned not to fear the others, their mental embrace, the merging of selves? The fear was gone, the revulsion, the primitive flight reaction. The joining itself remained, and now it was not a threat to her, no longer frightening; instead, it was warmer, dearer, sweeter, deeper than she could have imagined. She had an old, old wound of her own, as old as her service in Star Fleet, where a part of her had been torn away, and that wound had never really finally healed. Now at last that ancient pain had faded: wound to wound, the incomplete Onctiliian and the incomplete human had joined to form something far greater and more complete than either Earth or Onctiliis had ever seen before.

Chapter Ten

Spock stood on the beach, staring thoughtfully out to sea. "It seems to me, Captain," he said at last, "that the inconsistency between the Trellisanians' excessive concern for the well-being of others and their treatment of their slaves is highly significant."

Kirk, pacing back and forth along the narrow strip of sand between towering black cliffs, was giving Spock at best only half his attention. The other half was divided between chewing over their plans, looking for a major flaw, and wondering when their coconspirators would appear. "What's that, Mr. Spock?" he said absently.

"Their utter lack of concern for the slaves implies to me that they do not really consider those slaves much more than machines, or perhaps domesticated animals."

Kirk stopped pacing and looked at his Vulcan First Officer in astonishment. "Are you saying they're robots, Mr. Spock? Surely Dr. McCoy would have noticed that while treating the wounded."

"No, sir. You misunderstand me. I'm not saying that the slaves *are* machines. Indeed, matters would be simpler if they were. Rather, their masters seem to regard them as little better than machines—or animals, as I suggested. Only by adopting such a view of their slave class can the members of the ruling classes, such as Veedron, reconcile the wretched treatment of the slaves with this world's high-minded attitude toward other sapient beings in general."

"I'm not sure that follows, Mr. Spock. There have been many societies in Earth's history with slave classes. These were treated badly in many cases, but they were usually considered to be fully human."

Spock shook his head. "I must disagree with you, Captain. The ruling classes may have professed to consider those beneath them as human, but I doubt whether they really did. I'm convinced that Veedron and his equals do not so consider their slaves. If all goes well for us and Trellisane does indeed petition for membership in the Federation, that issue will come to the fore most painfully. Our actions here today—using the slave class to strike back at the Sealons, and encouraging them to look forward to full equality with their present masters—will simply have exacerbated the inevitable tensions when that day comes."

Kirk felt momentarily angry, but he responded in a calm voice. "That sounds like another criticism of me, Mr. Spock, for violating the Prime Directive."

Spock nodded slightly. "Yes, Captain. The Directive's wisdom becomes more apparent to me every time we behave in the proscribed manner."

Still keeping his voice calm, Kirk said, "Since the odds currently seem to favor Trellisane's destruction and a major, Galaxy-wide war, I suggest we postpone this abstract discussion for whatever future we might have."

Spock nodded again. "Indeed, Captain, logic seems to favor that course."

In spite of the determined pacifism of Trellisane, such jobs as mining and demolition demanded a supply of high explosives. Similarly, the world's high level of technology meant that the means to use those explosives for purposes other than mining and demolition—

to adapt them, for example, to warlike purposes—abounded. Most of the men most competent to do such a conversion were members of various technicians' and engineers' *gemots,* but not all. Often, a slave assistant to one of those technicians or engineers would be given enough responsibility to pick up a fair amount of pragmatic technical skill but would not be highly ranked enough to belong to a *gemot.* And among such assistants, some, Kirk had felt sure, would have been sufficiently badly treated to be as filled with resentment as the slave he and Spock had asked to bring them food in Veedron's headquarters building. Enough resentment, he hoped, to put their skills at his disposal.

At last he heard a faint crunch from the direction of one of the cliffs. The sound was repeated once, cautiously, and then grew to a succession of faint crunching noises. Footsteps, a group of men, headed toward them.

"Spock," he said softly. The Vulcan's alert pose showed that he had already heard the sound, probably long before the human had.

A small group, half a dozen men, all dressed in the nondescript, plain clothing Kirk had already come to associate with the slave class, came up to them. The newcomers looked over their shoulders furtively, clearly afraid that they would be caught and punished for what they were doing; they hung back from the two Star Fleet officers, their faces, even in the pale moonlight, betraying their distrust.

"Godor sent you?" Kirk asked them. Godor was the slave in Veedron's building, and Kirk had expected him to be with this group. "Where is he?"

They didn't answer him. After a few more uncertain glances about them, the group lost their faint courage and began to back away. A moment more, Kirk knew, and they would break and run, and that would be the end of all his hopes for resistance to the Sealons. He hesitated, uncharacteristically indecisive. If he spoke firmly to them, it might steel them, impart to them some of his own strength of will and determination, or it might just as likely panic them and send them running off all the faster.

Suddenly there were sounds of running feet from the other end of the beach. The group of Trellisanians froze for a moment in terror. Before they could flee, Kirk hissed at them, "It's only one man! Wait!" They hesitated.

Godor came up, panting, unable to speak, but his eyes blazed fiercely. He carried a large box under one arm. Kirk could tell from the way he handled it that the object was heavy; that the man would run with it showed his determination. Gulping for breath, Godor gasped out, "Here! What you wanted!" He stood still for a moment, waiting until breath came more easily, then said to the other Trellisanians, "Quickly, take us to your boat. Now you'll see what we can do!"

The other Trellisanians on the beach were a group of fishermen whom Godor had recruited earlier, after Kirk and Spock had explained to him what they would need to attack the Sealons. Now the fishermen grunted their acquiescence and led Godor and the two officers back in the direction from which they had approached minutes earlier.

"Captain," Spock said softly, "these men have not yet said a word to us."

Kirk nodded. "Yes. They'll talk treason to Godor, but we're strangers, and they still don't trust us. I hope they won't lose their nerve." He asked himself the question Spock had left unspoken: Have I really found rebels I can rely on?

The tide was rising; water lapped about the base of the wall of cliff the fishermen led them to. They walked through the ankle-deep water to skirt the cliffs, an occasional wave splashing up to their knees, and sometimes their waists, and breaking against the cliff face with a roar. Kirk staggered under the impact of one of the higher waves and would have fallen had Spock not caught his arm. "I'll take the seas of space," Kirk said, forcing a smile. He repressed the urge to tell their guides to hurry up, before the tide rose any higher. It was not so much the water itself that bothered him; the sea was generally calm, except for the occasional swell, the beach was still near, and he was a strong swimmer. Rather, it was the everpresent idea that the calm, rolling surface, with the moon marking a beautiful, silver trail upon it, hid the mysterious, deadly Sealons. This sea was suddenly not a friendly one. It belonged to the unseen enemy.

At last they reached an opening in the cliff face and turned inwards, away from the open sea, into a small cove where the water was even calmer. The moonlight flooded in through the opening in the cliff face, illuminating the small, concave beach and the large fishing boat pulled up on it.

Kirk pulled Godor aside and said to him, "Isn't there some kind of *gemot* to control fishing? Why do these men operate from this place instead of a built-up harbor?"

Godor shook his hand off. "Why do you care? Of course there's a *gemot,* and it doesn't allow men like these to own a boat or go fishing on their own. They have to work in secrecy, and sell their fish secretly."

Kirk grimaced. "I should have guessed. Do they understand that this might destroy their boat?"

"Yes. I explained that. Right now, they can't use it at all, because the Sealons destroy any boat that goes out far enough to reach the good fishing grounds. They have nothing to lose. I told them that when we've killed the Sealons, we'll join the Federation and destroy the *gemots,* and then they can have their pick of the fancy fishing boats in the harbors."

Kirk looked at him in astonishment but held his peace. After a pause, he said, "All right. Let's get that gadget loaded and push off."

They placed Godor's box carefully in the boat, and then Kirk, Spock, and Godor climbed in to adjust and set the mechanism contained in the box. When they were finished and straightened from their work, they found themselves alone on the beach. The fishermen's courage had deserted them at last, and they had silently faded away, using the hidden paths up the cliff face that only they knew. Godor cursed them for their desertion, but Kirk, in reaction to the controlled tension of the past hours, burst into a hearty laugh and could not make himself stop. Godor looked at him openmouthed, but Spock, raising one eyebrow, provided the needed verbal slap: "Sir, I must say that levity seems inappropriate."

Kirk sobered instantly. "Right as always, Spock. Now, if you'll climb out on the beach again and help me push this thing off the sand and into the water, I'll show you how to row a boat."

As they were straining against the boat's reluctant bulk, their feet slipping on the sand, Spock managed to gasp, "Surely, Captain, many rowers are required for a boat of this size."

Kirk, sweating heavily with the effort in the chill, damp air, grunted and said, "Star Fleet warned you that being first mate is a tough job, Mister."

Spock said nothing in reply. He threw his great Vulcan strength even more fully into the job and the boat, accelerating suddenly, slid the last few feet into the water and sat rocking gently on the slow swells of the sheltered cove. Kirk whooped with joy and waded into the waist-deep water and pulled himself over the side into the boat. Spock followed him, and as Kirk leaned over to offer him a hand to help, Spock was amazed to see that his captain's face wore a broad grin. It was something beyond simple levity or the release of long-suppressed tension, Spock thought; it seemed more the joy of a young boy on a long-awaited, long-delayed holiday. Spock's attitude toward naked human feelings had always been complex, a mixture of envy at the freedom humans possessed and revulsion at their lack of self-control. In James Kirk, he had found a human being he could admire, one who, with no Vulcan blood at all, seemed remarkably able to control his emotions for the sake of a higher goal, an integrated personality, a fine example of the ideal defined by an ancient Earth philosopher—"a life guided by reason and inspired by emotion." Now, suddenly, the control seemed to have disappeared. In this earnest, deadly business, James Kirk was behaving with boyish glee rather than the calm determination Spock might have expected. Kirk was dropping to the level of the average human, and Spock, who would have been greatly insulted had anyone suggested to him that he was capable of hero-worship, was deeply disturbed.

Dr. Leonard McCoy wrapped up his brief staff meeting at his operational headquarters and watched his Trellisanian assistants drag themselves from the room. No one had complained about the long hours and the psychological burden, but even without their obvious physical deterioration, McCoy could guess how they felt. Their feelings and state of health, he knew, matched his own. No, he thought, theirs was probably worse than his: he had at least the toughening effect of his Star Fleet background; no matter how deeply he might feel the pain of others, he had at least seen the effects of war so often that his reaction must be mild compared with that of these Trellisanian medical men.

The irony was that the current flood of victims would very soon abate, and it was *that* that worried him most. The bombardments from space had slackened and would probably soon stop. The Sealon ships that arrived now were more invasion craft, rather than attack ships; even the smaller ships that came to Trellisane from Sealon must be supply ships for the Sealon bases being built and expanded on the ocean floors, for the new spaceships landed in the seas rather than bothering with bombing runs against land targets. The current glut of bombing victims would probably be the end of it, and when they healed up enough to go home, the logistics of the situation would improve remarkably.

But McCoy was even more worried about the inevitable next stage. The psychological effects of the invasion were already appearing, and those were much harder to deal with. The *gemot* leaders seemed paralyzed by their loss of communication with their colleagues, and he suspected that paralysis would soon be followed by a deeper and more serious form of mental breakdown. But most of all he awaited with dread the apparently inevitable mass starvation his Trellisanian subordinates assured him was on its way. The world depended so heavily on food from the sea, that the loss of the oceans to the Sealons would probably prove to be a mortal blow.

Once, before realizing how futile it was, McCoy had exploded at them. "Well then, why not *do* something about it, damn it all! Start right now with extensive agricultural programs and food rationing. And attack the Sealons on the sea bottoms. For God's sake, let's take the fight to them! You can't just roll over and die!"

But they could do just that; they almost seemed to want to do it. McCoy's own organization was virtually the only functioning government left on the planet. It was, however, not that disorganization that gave him most of his problems, but rather the Trellisanian nature itself: malleable, retiring, timid, and so excessively humane that they would rather suffer pain from their enemies than inflict it.

The war between the two worlds—if "war" was even the right word, given the lack of any Trellisanian defense—reminded McCoy painfully of the time James Kirk had been split into two beings by a transporter malfunction. One had been the beast, the wolf in every man, the animal left in us from our most primitive days, amoral, wanting only the satiation of every desire. The other being had been the softer side of man, what Spock had called "the positive side"; but it had been unable to make decisions, especially the harder, less humane ones. Together, the two beings were the remarkable and admirable Captain James T. Kirk; apart, neither could survive for long, and both had come near to dying before a transporter repair had made it possible to recombine them. He saw Trellisane and Sealon as the same sort of division: one society overly bestial, the other overly humane. And perhaps both were doomed if they could not somehow unite, unlikely as any such union looked now. Sealon, probably, would complete the destruction of Trellisane and would then be itself destroyed by Klingon.

McCoy sighed, put his arms on the table, and leaned his head on them for a moment's rest. Beneath the cynic was the hopeful romantic, but this time cynicism seemed more justified. Pessimism, rather. Unity through diversity, he thought as he drifted away into sleep. That's what that pointy-eared, green-blooded walking computer likes to espouse. What does he know about it? If he could convince the Sealons and the Trellisanians to try it . . . His dreams were filled with explosions and blood.

Far from shore, surrounded only by the gently swelling, moonlit ocean, the three men in the fishing boat waited tensely for an explosion to end their own voyage in blood. They had already journeyed further from the shore without being detected and destroyed by the Sealons beneath them than Spock had predicted they would. The oars had been wrapped in cloths to muffle their sound, in the small hope that this would make the Sealons' detection devices and computers dismiss them as insignificant. They had not spoken to each other except in an occasional whisper.

Now they halted and sat still in the boat for a few minutes. Spock had laid his tricorder at his feet and, at regular intervals during their trip away from the shore, had pointed it downwards. Now he did so again. "Well?" Kirk whispered. "Anything stronger here?"

"Yes, Captain. The earlier readings indicated the fringes of a base beneath us, but now we must be near the center. The readings may not be reliable through this depth of water, but the density of life forms and machinery here is remarkable."

Kirk could almost hear McCoy's voice muttering, "Long-winded son-of-a-gun, isn't he?" Kirk's own euphoria continued, had even increased since they'd left the shore, and he grinned at the imagined conversation. "Let's get this overboard," he whispered, pointing at the box at their feet.

The three of them picked up Godor's box and, all leaning over the side together and ignoring the extreme tilt this gave to the boat, they lowered it onto the calm surface of the water and let it go. With only a faint splash, it sank beneath the surface and dropped quickly out of sight. "Row!" Kirk ordered. He and Spock grabbed their oars and bent their backs to the task, while Godor kept nervously scanning the water's surface for Sealons. Had all the fishermen been with them, as Kirk had planned, they could have made good speed, but as it was, the boat moved away from the site of their primitive depth-charge with agonizing slowness.

An enormous concussion slammed the boat upwards. Kirk and Spock were tumbled from their seats onto the boards, but Godor, who had been half standing to see further, shot out of the boat into the water. He surfaced instantly, his face filled with terror, and screamed wordlessly at them.

Kirk gathered himself quickly and dove in. He swam to Godor, who was still screaming, and who now looked at Kirk with blank fear and tried to keep him away. Cursing, Kirk grabbed the Trellisanian's clothing with his left hand and punched him savagely on the jaw with his right. Godor's eyes rolled upwards and he went slack in the water. Pulling him by the hair, Kirk drew him back toward the boat. Spock drew them both back onboard.

"I would recommend warp speed, Captain," Spock said, calmly picking up his oar again. Kirk granted him one brief look of surprise, but picked up his own oar and began rowing vigorously without comment. Spock's rare attempts at humor, he thought, came at strange times, almost as if the Vulcan wanted to point out to his human companions just how immune he was to panic or any other overemotional reaction to circumstances.

Behind them, the sea heaved itself up in a huge bubble that turned white and then exploded into a fountain of spray. It rose high into the air and then rained down on the surface of the sea and into their boat, almost swamping them. Unidentifiable bits of metal pattered on the water and the boat and its occupants. Something much like a human hand landed on Kirk's lap. Half repelled, half fascinated, he picked it up and stared at it.

"Webbed," Spock observed quietly. "We seem to have found our target."

Suddenly overcome with disgust, Kirk threw the hand overboard and began rowing again. "Let's get the Hell out of here, Spock," he said through gritted teeth.

The slave's name was Spenreed. His friends had brought him to McCoy, and he was suffering from nothing more than a minor leg wound that had become infected. It was bad enough by now, though, that he couldn't put any weight on the leg and needed support from a fellow slave on each side, and he was drowsy, obviously having trouble with clouded thoughts. Clearly, without treatment he would die quite soon. McCoy had already deduced that slaves were generally not given treatment, except in those rare cases where they were both vital and irreplaceable; in most cases, though, the vast pool of replacements made it easier to let them die. I wonder if we're fighting on the right side, he kept asking himself. I don't see how the Sealons can be any more callous than this.

Word of McCoy's treating slaves' wounds had got around, following the branches of one of those mysterious grapevines that slave classes always seem to develop on any planet and in any age. As a result, more and more of them were bringing sick or injured fellows to him. He could usually fit them in, leaving his Trellisanian assistants to take care of the patients who weren't slaves. It couldn't continue, of course: as word spread further, he'd quickly be overwhelmed; after all, his assistants would refuse in horror to help him in this work, were he to make the mistake of asking them.

McCoy followed what had become his usual practice. He beckoned Spenreed's bearers to follow him with their burden, and he led them into a small operating room, lined with shelves, where they would be uninterrupted. This had been a storeroom before McCoy's appearance. The two slaves helped Spenreed onto the table, and McCoy applied the hypospray to his arm. Spenreed went under immediately. Whistling, McCoy set to work on cleaning and dressing the leg wound. Of the two slaves, standing by the operating table, only one turned pale. The other watched what McCoy was doing with interest. McCoy grunted. "Look carefully. Maybe you'll be this world's first slave surgeon." The slave grinned and nodded.

Making sure the slave was watching what he was doing, McCoy opened up Spenreed's head. Gently, he reached a microprobe into the brain and extracted a small capsule. He held it up for the openmouthed slave to see, then closed Spenreed up again. He busily applied glue and synthetic skin, then reached over to the nearby wall and dropped the capsule onto a shelf, into the dozen or so that were already scattered there.

The watching slave clenched his jaw. "Three days after birth, our children are taken away for a medical examination. The defective ones aren't brought back. The others . . ." He bent his head toward the scattering of capsules.

McCoy nodded. "Um-hmm." He used the hypospray again, and Spenreed opened his eyes, groaned, and struggled to sit up. "How do you feel?" McCoy asked him.

Spenreed groaned again. "I've got a headache," he complained.

McCoy chuckled. "You shouldn't. I just exorcised you."

Chapter Eleven

Security couldn't pull itself together. If Kinitz had had one serious failing, it was his inability to delegate authority properly. He had had two prime assistants, either of whom could have taken over Security section upon his death, but both were now unconscious and close to death in Medical. Beyond them, Kinitz had not provided for command in case of his death, for that situation—his defeat and death—had been simply unimaginable to him. That personality flaw of overconfidence had proved to be his fatal one.

Now a power struggle was underway in Security section. The surviving subordinates, all nominally of equal rank, were squabbling, each trying to assert his own claim to temporary command. They needed a strong-willed superior to enforce order upon them, and now Kinitz was gone. The matter could have been settled quickly enough by an appeal to the bridge, and they tried that, but the bridge was strangely uncommunicative. Calls up there were always answered by Sulu, who they knew had the con in the captain's absence, and he consistently refused to issue an order that would halt the confusion. "Wait until the alert is over" was all they could get out of him.

Kinitz would have been made suspicious by this, but

the men struggling for control of Security were not. Nor did they correlate Sulu's unresponsiveness with the escape of their prisoners. Star Fleet Security's recruitment and training emphasized physical strength and competence and an unquestioning acceptance of a superior's orders; original thought was not a Security man's strong point.

Chief Engineer Scott uttered a mighty curse and slammed his hand down onto the metal housing of the warp reactor monitoring computer. One of his assistants, working nearby, looked at him in amazement and almost asked for a translation into English of Scott's exclamation, but then thought better of it and went on silently with his work.

Scott had caught the glance, however. "Aye, you may well ask, lad," he grumbled. "Here we are heading off somewhere under warp drive, leaving the captain down there in the middle of a war, and Mr. Sulu up on the bridge won't tell me what's going on. The alert's still on, and I don't understand that, either. I've asked for permission to turn it off for a few hours for maintenance, and he won't even let me do that! I can't get a straight answer out of him. I've a mind to go up there myself and force it out of him."

His subordinate was appalled. "But, sir, there's a Red Alert on! You're supposed to stay here."

Scott snorted in disgust. "An alert! That's fishy, too, I'm telling you. I've decided. I'm going up there and put a stop to all this right now." He listened to the faint sounds of the laboring warp drive reactor and shook his head in mixed annoyance and concern. He didn't need the monitoring computer to tell him all was not well. He headed for the exit, grumbling to himself, and made for the nearest elevator. As soon as it opened, he stepped in and snapped "Bridge!" at it, putting all his frustration and anger into the word.

A computer's voice replied: "Bridge has been declared closed to all personnel not on duty there now."

"Och, you stupid—" Scott stopped and brought himself under control. "This is the chief engineer, and this is an emergency. I'm *ordering* you to override that and take me to the bridge." After a pause, as if the decision were a painful one, the elevator lurched into motion. Scott rebuked himself for taking his feelings out on the machine, which was doing no more than following the orders of fallible humans. He suppressed the desire to utter an apology. He liked certain people, and he liked certain brands of Scotch whiskey and some brandies, but he liked virtually every machine he had ever encountered.

When the elevator reached the bridge level, the doors refused to open. The computer spoke again, almost sounding apologetic this time: "Bridge is closed." Scott could almost imagine it adding, "Sure you don't want to reconsider?"

He lost his temper again. "You know my voiceprint. Open the damned door!"

The doors swished open this time, and Scott stormed out onto the bridge. "Mr. Sulu," he bellowed, "I want to know just what's—" Too late to retreat, he saw the phasers leveled at him from all sides. Someone he didn't know sat in the captain's chair and stared at him appraisingly. "Who are you?" this stranger said coolly.

Scott forgot the phasers and strode forward until he stood next to the captain's chair. "Who are *you*, that's what I want to know, and what's going on up here? Why are you in that chair?"

"Scotty." Sulu's voice, tired, defeated. Scott turned toward him, disturbed to find that Sulu, who he had been told was to have the con, was on the bridge though obviously not in command. "Scotty, just cooperate with them."

Scott looked around and measured the situation.

Strangers, all armed and all alert, and all looking at him hostilely. The bridge crew sitting slumped at their stations, all looking as tired and defeated as Sulu sounded. Uhura looked up at him, her gaze dull, almost without recognition, and then she turned back to her communications console. Only Chekov showed anything approaching liveliness, and even that was far less than he had learned to expect from the young Russian. Scott did a quick mental calculation. If he remembered the latest duty roster correctly, most of these people shouldn't even be here, should have gone off duty hours ago. He turned back to the man in the command chair and glared at him. "Okay, mister, I'll tell you that I'm the chief engineer of this ship, and now you'd better talk."

Hander Morl, to his own surprise, felt intimidated, in spite of the four armed killers on the bridge who were at his instant beck and call. He couldn't show that, however, or his control over this ship would become even more precarious than he feared it already was. He smiled at Scott calmly, superciliously, and told him just who he was. "I'm in control of this ship, Engineer," he said, "and in not too many hours, I'm going to take it into the Romulan Neutral Zone and start a war."

"A war! Good God, man!" Scott took a deep breath and tried again. "Now let me tell you what's really going to happen. Our speed is already dropping, and it's going to keep on dropping. If we're all lucky, this ship will come to a stop and drop out of warp into normal space. If we're all unlucky, the whole scow will disappear in a cloud of vapor when the warp reactor blows. I've got repairs to do! I've been calling up here to tell you that, and I've been getting doubletalk." He glared at Morl. "And I suppose you were behind that, too."

Morl licked his lips, ignoring the chief engineer. He muttered, "We can't stop. Or slow down." Suddenly he stood up and pointed his phaser at Chekov. His voice shook with rage. "You! You must have known we were slowing down, and you didn't tell me!"

"You didn't ask me," Chekov said sweetly. He reminded himself that he had always wondered what it felt like to die by phaser; it looked like he was about to find out.

The Nactern warrior with whom Chekov had been so unsuccessful earlier stepped between him and Morl and said firmly, "Don't be a fool, Hander. You know we need him. A small delay won't hurt."

Sulu flashed him a quick look, but Chekov kept his face impassive. Perhaps, he thought, his investment was already paying dividends.

Morl sat down in the command chair again, trembling from the reaction to his own anger but also from a sudden fear that all was going to end in disaster after all. "Let me think," he whispered. Could he take the chance of continuing as they were? The man obviously knew his job—Morl respected the capabilities of Star Fleet personnel, even if he thought their motives smacked of cowardice. If the ship blew up, nothing would have been gained; Morl and his people would have died without purpose, without starting the war. Even if the warp engines blew or failed without destroying the ship, they'd be reduced to impulse power, and Morl knew that it would take months or even years to reach the Neutral Zone. They might be caught and stopped long before that. Everything was falling apart! His grand plan, the wonderful opportunity this fortuitous seizure of one of Star Fleet's proudest vessels had provided—it had seemed at first as if the Fates themselves were on the side of the United Expansion Party, as indeed Morl had always thought they were. Now he was faced with failure no matter which course he took.

He licked his lips again. "How long would that maintenance you mentioned take?" he asked Scott, and he couldn't keep the uncertainty and fear he felt from showing in his voice.

Scott smiled slightly. "Two hours. Maybe three. Mind you," he added, holding up a cautioning hand, "if there are certain parts that need replacement, well, then, it could take a day or more."

A day or more! Impossible that he could keep control of the bridge for that long! Morl's suspicious nature asserted itself. Was the man lying? How would Morl be able to find out even if he were? Then he noticed that his own subordinates were watching him, disturbed at his indecisiveness. So were the *Enterprise* personnel, becoming alert and hopeful again as they thought they saw a weakness in their captors. "All right," he snapped, his voice firm. "All right, Engineer. I'll allow that maintenance, but no replacements that take too long. I want you done with the whole thing in three hours at the outside." Scott turned to go. "Wait a minute!" Morl shouted. "You think I'm a fool? You're not going back down there alone!" He hesitated for a moment more, then gestured to one of the Assassins. "You'll go with him," he told the man. "Keep an eye on him all the time so he doesn't betray us. Keep your phaser hidden, but be ready. Don't let him talk to anyone else down there except for the technical matters." He turned to Scott. "As for you, remember that I have all these people here under my control. If you try to pull anything, I'll kill them. All of them."

Scott looked around at the bridge crew, his face grim. "I'll remember," he said. He stared wordlessly at Morl for a moment. "I'm not about to forget about you, you can be sure of that." He strode back toward the elevator, the Assassin close behind him.

Only minutes later, the faint lurch of transition between normal space and subspace, more psychological than physical, hit Morl. On the great screen in front of him, the star field disappeared momentarily and then shimmered back into existence. But now it was static, the motion apparent because of the enormous velocities of the higher warp speeds utterly absent. The illusion of a flowing universe had given way to the illusion that the ship was absolutely still in a static universe. Although Morl ordered Sulu to press on at the greatest speed the impulse engines would provide, he knew that those speeds were so low in comparison to the vast distance yet to be covered, that the *Enterprise* might as well be standing still. Their pursuers, if there were any, would surely not be so limited. It must have happened when the ship was damaged and he and his partners had escaped. Why had the fool let his ship be damaged that way? If Morl had been in charge already, it would never have happened! But it had happened. Morl groaned.

He was too preoccupied to notice the rush of hope that had buoyed up the slumping Sulu. He knew from his console that the ship's speed had been constant before, under warp drive. Scott had lied, quickly and extemporaneously, but apparently convincingly. Now they had gained a few hours, another ally in the form of the chief engineer, and their captors had been weakened by one. It had taken a lot to make Sulu's natural cheerfulness go dormant; now it came bubbling up again.

Chapter Twelve

At the sound of a throat being cleared, McCoy looked up from report from an assistant he was reading. Spenreed stood in the doorway, looking stricken. "Doctor. I wanted to thank you for helping me. I'm— My call has come."

"Your what?"

"My, uh, my call. So you won't see me again."

"I don't understand," McCoy said. "You're going somewhere?"

Spenreed choked back a sudden sob. "No. No, I'm not. *Yegemot* don't go anywhere. We just die."

"Die!" McCoy thought he began to understand. "Are you trying to tell me you've received some sort of premonition of death?"

Spenreed nodded. "The call. I was officially informed by a representative of the Food Provenders *gemot*. He said it must be before the banquet for *gemot* leaders."

"Oh, yes. That damned banquet. I have to be there, and I'm sure not looking forward to it. Now, you listen to me, Spenreed. I've run into this sort of superstition, this fortune telling and forecasting men's deaths, on other worlds, and I can tell you it's nonsense. It doesn't matter where in the Galaxy you run into it, it's still nonsense. You come to me after that banquet, and I'll repeat everything I just said, and we'll see how you feel about it then."

Spenreed laughed suddenly and grinned a fierce, broad grin. "You may see me at the banquet, Doctor. Tell me then." He stalked off down the hall, leaving McCoy to wonder at his sudden anger.

McCoy pondered both that anger and the rest of the curious episode for some minutes. Finally, he shook his head and dismissed it all. "Damned ignorance," he muttered. Maybe I can force-feed some science into these slaves. If their masters don't object. Well, their masters better learn very soon to change their attitudes, because if Trellisane joins the Federation, things are going to be very different on this world. And speaking of feeding, he thought, how the Hell can I get these people to start growing their own food on the land? Now that the seas are lost to them, or soon will be, they've got to stop depending on those sea plants supplemented by fish meat. Maybe they're going to cut down on what they feed the slaves, to make what's left go further. Damned if I'll stand for that.

He shook his head in annoyance and then forced his attention back to the report on his desk.

Their success emboldened the fishermen. Groups of them set out in their boats with explosive devices delivered to them by Godor. He refused to tell Kirk and Spock who made these for him. As foreigners, they were obviously still not entirely to be trusted; who knew if, the present crisis being over, they would not betray Godor and the other conspirators to their masters, despite all their fine talk now about the Federation and its rules of equality. This was maddening to Kirk, for he knew how fickle war is. Godor went out on the boats often, success having returned all of his courage and more, and it was inevitable that the Sealons would eventually strike back. If Godor was lost, Kirk would have no further access to the explosives.

Spock agreed with him, something that had become unusual. "Indeed, Captain, the Sealons' quiescence so far is surprising. I can only assume that they have been preoccupied with plans for the next stage of their invasion. Perhaps they expected more resistance than they encountered in fact. That would explain why they landed in the deeper waters, rather than along the continental margin. Now that they have gained confidence from the lack of any Trellisanian response, they are probably planning to move their installations wholesale into the shallower water. We must have caught them at that stage, and they have tried to ignore us so far. That cannot continue."

"Yes, I'm sure that's true." They were on the same beach where their small resistance movement had started, waiting for the return of a boat carrying a depth charge. Kirk looked at his timepiece. "It's taking them a long time," he muttered. "Ah, there!" Out on the horizon, the water rose up in a dome that exploded upwards into a fountain of spray. Some distance from the site of the underwater explosion, the boat showed as a small speck on the surface of the sea. Kirk could imagine the fishermen rowing frantically away from the explosion.

Spock, watching the boat too, squinted and said, "Captain, something in the water . . ."

"I can't see as well as you can, Spock." But then even he could see it: things in the water around the boat, furious splashings. He could barely see the movements as the fishermen tried to beat the attackers away with their oars. The shapes swarmed over the sides into the boat, overwhelming the Trellisanians. Then there was a mass movement back over the sides into the sea, almost a liquid pouring, as if the attackers were boneless and they had reduced their victims to the same state. In minutes, only the empty boat was left, bobbing up and down on the waves still spreading outwards from the explosion. "So much for them ignoring us, Spock."

"Captain, if the Sealons had chosen simply to eliminate the threat, they could have destroyed the fishing boat from beneath, from a distance, without attacking the crew directly. That was the nature of their previous attacks upon Trellisanian merchant vessels, and it entails far less risk to themselves."

"You seem to think they must have had more in mind this time than defense."

Spock nodded. "Indeed, sir. I would guess they wish to interrogate. Our attacks upon them have been atypical; they break the pattern. The Sealons, or perhaps their Klingon masters, would wish to know what has caused this change."

The two turned away from the sea and began to walk slowly up the beach. The sun was bright, and the white-yellow sand reflected it back into their faces. "It's probably pointless to send out any more boats, now," Kirk said. "We'll have to come up with something else. If they really are preparing to move closer to the land, it becomes even more difficult."

"Captain!" Spock said sharply. "Listen!"

In the distance, some sort of sea bird was wheeling about in the air above the cliff face, uttering an unpleasant high-pitched cry. From behind came the steady lapping of waves on the shore. Beyond that, Kirk could hear nothing. Knowing how acute a Vulcan's hearing was, however, he stood still and strained his ears. "Well, Mr. Spock?"

Spock shook his head. "I'm sorry, Captain. I was sure I heard voices. Very faint and muffled. Wait! There it is again."

This time, even Kirk could hear something, though it sounded more like the cry of an animal, and muffled, than a human voice. He thought the sound had come from the base of the cliffs to their left. Then it was answered from behind. Kirk spun around, but at first he could see nothing. The sun, dazzling off the sand and water, almost blinded him.

Shapes rose from the water and shambled onto the sand. They were bulky, shapeless, larger than a man, and they called back and forth to each other eagerly, with something vicious in the sound. The calls were repeated from the directions of the cliffs at either end of the beach.

"Quickly, Captain, before they can cut us off!" Spock began to run toward the rising land where the beach ended and the undergrowth of the interior began. Following him, Kirk told himself, at least they probably can't move fast on land.

Something hit him, like a great electric shock coursing through every nerve pathway simultaneously, flinging him forward onto his face. Paralyzed, limp as a rag doll, his limbs flopping helplessly, Kirk rolled a couple of times and ended up on his left side, facing toward the water. He was still half conscious, but he couldn't regain the slightest control over his body. A phaser of some sort, he thought. On low stun. Even without being able to turn and look, he knew Spock must be lying not too many meters away, in the same condition.

Kirk's eyes were open. He hadn't the power to close them even if he had wanted to. Helplessly, he watched the Sealons—he had never had any doubt, from the first instant, that that was what these creatures were— struggle across the sand toward him. He could tell that they were making as much speed as they could, perhaps afraid that Kirk's followers would show up to rescue him. Before he had sensed both viciousness and triumph; now he caught the hint of something unstoppable, of a driving force that knew no moral restraint. Kirk struggled without success to move his arms and legs. His body was as paralyzed as ever.

The first Sealon to reach him reared itself up over

him, one arm raised, and Kirk prepared himself mentally for the crushing blow that would end his life. But apparently it was only a signal to the others, for the creature lowered its arm again without harming Kirk, and the others began to appear within his field of vision.

The creatures' colors ranged from pale brown to almost black. Their skin seemed to be covered by short, wiry hairs, covering them like a shield. Their general shape seemed humanoid, but he could see webbing between the fingers and toes. They were obviously heavily muscled, beneath a surface layer of fat. Their legs were short and apparently unable to support them well on land. He couldn't turn his head to see more, so he was unable to see what their faces looked like.

He was grasped roughly by powerful hands and lifted. His body sagged, his arms, legs, and head flopping from side to side as they carried him back toward the water. Had they spared him so far only to let him drown helplessly, unable to control his limbs and swim?

Just before they reached the water, however, his head was grasped and something opaque was forced over his face. He couldn't resist in any way; no control had yet returned. Straps were tightened around the back of his head to keep the device in place. The opacity was complete; he was in utter blackness. But he could feel water lapping over him and then rising up over his head. The hands still grasped him, pulling him deeper and deeper under the ocean he could not see.

McCoy was trying without success to find someone who could and would assume responsibility for food distribution. None of this fell within the scope of the duties McCoy had volunteered for, but what little government Trellisane had had seemed to have entirely disappeared, and he knew he couldn't just ignore matters and let starvation creep up on them. There must be someone—or some *gemot*—who dealt with food storage and so on, and if he could only find them, he could perhaps talk them into trying to forestall the inevitable. Was it the Food Provenders he'd heard references to? But no one he questioned seemed to know or care who had the responsibility. Much as he admired the humane attitudes of Trellisane—at least, during peace time—and what little of their art and culture he had happened to see, McCoy was beginning to have strong doubts whether this world could be saved. Surely the natives must contribute to the effort too!

It was while he was pondering this mixture of practical and abstract problems that Veedron stalked into his small office and confronted him. This was a face of Trellisane McCoy had not seen before: angry and imperious, and chastising. "Those friends of yours," Veedron snapped. "They've done something to anger the Sealons!"

McCoy's astonishment gave way to an anger of his own. "Anger the Sealons! What are you talking about? They're invading your world, killing your people! Whatever Jim and Spock are doing against them is what you should be doing."

"No!" Veedron yelled. "You're wrong! If we don't do anything to fight back, they'll realize how foolish they're being to do this, and they'll stop and go home."

"Do you really believe that? Even after what they've already done to your world?"

"Yes, Dr. McCoy. Yes, I do. They'll leave, and then everything will be the way it was, the way it should be. Everyone on Trellisane will settle back into his rightful place and be happy with it."

For the first time, McCoy became aware of the terrible fear underlying Veedron's bluster. He spoke calmly, gently to the Trellisanian, trying to ease that fear. "I'm sure Jim and Spock know the dangers. We've dealt with interplanetary wars before, Veedron. You simply can't try to win by letting your enemy destroy your world. That never has—"

"Your friends are destroying this world!" Veedron interrupted. "It won't matter even if the Sealons leave. After what those two have started, things will never be the same again."

"There's a great deal of destruction to repair, of course," McCoy said soothingly, feeling puzzled by Veedron's near hysteria, "but if we can just end this war and get back in contact with Star Fleet, the Federation will help you rebuild."

"But it's not the destruction, not the buildings." Veedron's voice cracked. "It's our *society* they're breaking down. After this, the slaves . . . the slaves will swallow us whole."

"The slaves!" The real cause of Veedron's fear began to become apparent at last. Things he had seen during the last two days but had ignored began to coalesce for McCoy. "I think I've been too preoccupied," he muttered.

Veedron flopped into a chair. "Oh, you offworlders just don't understand how things are here, how things have to be in order to have a civilized planet! You have all those other species from all over your domains, who look so different from you, to do your work for you. You don't have to face the moral and ethical burdens we have running this world."

McCoy burst out laughing. "If you only knew how much you sound like some very old relatives of mine back home! Sit still, my good man. I've got a lot to tell you about how the Federation operates. I don't think you're going to like all of it."

Veedron looked at him with distaste, but he made no move to escape.

The pressure on Kirk's body increased steadily. He yawned desperately, stretching his jaws inside the flexible breathing mask the Sealons had fitted over his face, hoping he was avoiding damage to his eardrums. Only after he had been doing this for some minutes did he realize that the paralysis was wearing off. He jerked his arms free of the hands holding them and kicked in what he thought was the direction of the surface. He couldn't spare the time to take his mask off so that he could see the light of the surface. Something hard hit him on the back of the head, stunning him and stopping his escape. Strong hands gripped his arms and legs again and started pulling him along once more. Another heavy blow to the back of the head, and his consciousness faded.

When Kirk recovered consciousness, he was first aware of a grotesque headache and next that he was lying on a hard, dry surface and was surrounded by warm air rather than cold water. He couldn't quite focus his eyes.

"Captain." Spock's voice. Nearby, and full of concern. "Jim. Are you functional?"

Kirk suppressed a mad urge to giggle. "Yes, Mr. Spock," he said, the words coming out in a slur. He could hardly control his tongue, and he could still make no more than a blur out of his surroundings. "I'm adequately functional."

"Here, Captain," Spock said. "Have some of this."

Kirk's head was raised and something was placed against his lips. He sipped a hot liquid, acrid both to taste and smell. He forced a few sips down, and his headache faded and his vision cleared. He could see Spock leaning over him, looking at his face with concern. As soon as Spock realized his captain could now see him, the look of concern disappeared, quickly replaced by the normal impenetrable Vulcan stolidity.

From Kirk's right, a harsh voice spoke. "Captain Kirk. You're lucky they didn't crush your skull. A Sealon is very strong, and it isn't wise to make them angry."

Kirk pushed himself shakily to his feet and squinted in the direction of the voice. A Klingon stood there, trying to mask his arrogance and hostility behind an assumption of polite interest. "Aha," Kirk said. "At last we find the puppet masters."

The Klingon flushed, his false politeness vanishing. He growled, the sound of a beast, the strange, almost instinctual hatred between Klingons and humans nearly overmastering him. With an effort, he assumed his mask again. With an even greater effort, he smiled at the two Star Fleet officers. "We know who you are. Captain James Tiberius Kirk of the *U.S.S. Enterprise*, and the ship's science officer and first officer, the Vulcan, Spock. We could tell from what our other captives . . . uh, *revealed* to us that you two were behind the sudden eruption of resistance. We advised the Sealons to capture you so that the resistance would end."

"You 'advised' them, you said?" Kirk said. "Wouldn't 'ordered' be the right word?"

The Klingon smirked. "I think you're missing the whole point, Kirk. We're here merely in an advisory rôle. It's obvious to us which of these two races is the more qualified to rule this star system. It must be obvious to you, too. If we're doing anything, it's only to help the Sealons in their natural progress to mastery. It's *they* who expressed the natural and proper desire to expand and conquer; we only provided the means. You have no right to complain if we chose to back the stronger faction and your faction loses."

"Sir," Spock said, in that dry tone that alerted Kirk to the beginning of a theoretical disquisition, "the distinction you have drawn is surely moot. The Trellisanians provided the Sealons with space flight, it is true, but they did not teach them to arm their ships. Nor did they provide them with phasers; indeed, that is a device the Sealons, as an underwater culture, would surely not have originated on their own and would not have desired or known how to use. It was not until your own intervention that the possibility of attacking and invading Trellisane arose. By creating that possibility, you in effect led the Sealons into their present path. Klingon must be held accountable for the present war—if not in the eyes of the Organians, then in the view of the Federation Council. There will surely be retribution."

The Klingon officer laughed at Spock. "Vulcan, in a few days, it won't matter what rôle we played. When the Sealons move onto the land, your weak friends will be killed off, and then it will be too late for the Organians or the Federation government to do anything about it."

"Correction," Kirk said. "In a few days, you can expect a Romulan fleet to arrive and take over this system."

The Klingon whirled on him, his hand dropping to the phaser on his belt. "What? What lie is this? Speak quickly, Kirk, or you're dead!"

Kirk grinned at him, deliberately goading him into losing his temper. They were alone in the office with the Klingon, and if he could force the officer into acting hastily, moving within range of them, he and Spock could surely disarm him. But the Klingon seemed to realize his danger, and he stepped back again, drew his phaser, and held it aimed at a point in the air midway between Kirk and Spock. "Now, Kirk," he said in a voice held deliberately calm, "explain what you mean."

Kirk hesitated. There was no longer any security reason for not telling this Klingon the whole story; it was rather that he felt a great reluctance at admitting how he had lost his ship. "A group of fanatics have managed to take over the *Enterprise,* and they're on their way right now to the Romulan Neutral Zone, hoping to attack a Romulan vessel or base and start a war between them and the Federation."

The Klingon laughed uproariously. "The great Captain Kirk has lost his ship!" he shouted. "Wonderful! Why should that worry us, Kirk? You've destroyed your career, and now your stupid Federation and the Romulans will destroy each other. That's good news for us—the best possible. With both of you eliminated, there'll be no one to stand in our way."

Spock said, "Sir, you underestimate the Romulans. They will quite possibly manage to capture the *Enterprise* without destroying it, and then they will find out from the crew what has been happening here. Even if they do destroy the *Enterprise*, they will surely wonder why the Federation would initiate a war with them by sending a lone ship to attack their empire. In that case, they will surely become suspicious that something quite different is underway and will explore the star systems in the neighborhood of the Neutral Zone to try to determine what it is. In either case, they will be greatly angered to find that Klingon is trying to encroach in this area, which they regard as something of a no-man's-land between the three spheres of influence. That is precisely why the Federation has moved so cautiously here. Klingon has made a serious mistake by not emulating us. I doubt that your empire is prepared at this point to undertake a war against the Romulans and the Federation—or more properly, the Organians—at the same time."

The Klingon glared at Spock for a moment, obviously wanting to find the words to destroy the Vulcan's argument but unable to do so. "Why should I believe any of this?" he asked finally.

Before Spock could generously explain why, logically, he was not obliged to believe it, Kirk broke in. "You can check on the whereabouts of the *Enterprise* quickly enough."

The Klingon thought for a moment, then called in a guard from outside, another Klingon, and left the room quickly. After some minutes, he returned looking shaken. "The base on Sealon verifies some of what you've said," he told them, his manner almost friendly. "The Invasion Commandant wants you both sent to him on Sealon so he can discuss what to do next. If it were up to me, I'd kill you both instead of cooperating with you."

"And me without my swimsuit," Kirk said. Invasion Commandant, he thought. At least they're being honest with themselves about what they're doing.

Chapter Thirteen

As if completely unaware of the Assassin looking over his shoulder, Lieutenant Commander Montgomery Scott, chief engineer of the *U.S.S. Enterprise,* pulled his head from the crawl space beside the main warp reactor and muttered, "Well, Scotty my boy, that's probably the best you can do without replacing those parts." Shaking his head, he walked across the open space in the center of Engineering Section to the warp reactor monitoring computer and stood in front of it clucking his tongue.

The Assassin had followed, moving soundlessly. "What's wrong?" he asked, outwardly unperturbed but in fact disturbed by Scott's obvious worry.

"Hmm? Oh, it's you. Well, y'see, I've done the maintenance your boss so kindly permitted me to. Now at least we won't blow up when the drive fails. But it'll still fail unless I'm allowed to remove some parts from the reactor and completely replace them. And he won't allow me time for that."

"How long before it gives out?"

Scott shrugged elaborately. "No way of knowing— until it happens. No one tests the things that way, because a *real* starship captain knows enough to let his chief engineer have his way where the engines are concerned."

The Assassin said impatiently, "Just so they last long enough to get us to the Romulans."

Scott forced his anger down. The thought that his beloved engines—and the ship itself—were only tools to these madmen infuriated him. They would let his ship be destroyed, and for no purpose other than their own madness! Still, he could tell that if he attacked this man he would accomplish nothing except to get himself crippled or killed. He could do the ship and the Federation more good by keeping himself in working condition until some sort of opportunity presented itself.

One of Scott's assistants strolled into the room at that moment, his arm cradling a clipboard on which he was checking off various status points as he verified proper operations. He stopped in surprise when he saw his chief. "Sir, I thought you went off duty a couple of hours ago."

"Just finished the warp engine maintenance, Bill," Scott told him, hoping the young man would have the wit to accept that explanation for now.

Instead, the young engineer frowned and looked over the papers on his clipboard. "But none of that was scheduled, sir. I thought I remembered that we took care of that last week."

"Right. That was the regular maintenance. We had bad problems because of the shaking up the engines took during that attack at the beginning of the Red Alert."

"Oh, yes, sir, I see." Diligently and scrupulously, the young man wrote a few remarks on his check-off list. "In that case, sir, I'd better look it over so I know what to tell the man who relieves me." And before Scott could think of the right words to stop him without making the Assassin suspicious, the engineer had stuck his own head into the crawl space, still uncovered, that Scott had vacated only minutes before.

Scott stole a quick glance at the Assassin. The man was watching the younger engineer and flexing his hands unconsciously. Scott sensed immediately that his assistant was close to death, and he said, in a cheerful tone, "We'd better get back to the bridge, now, and tell them that we're done down here." But the Assassin motioned him to silence.

The young engineer came out of the crawl space frowning. "But, sir—"

"Yes, yes, lad, I know," Scott cut in. "Those parts need to be replaced, or they'll give out soon. But with this alert on, the bridge just won't give me the time to do that." Star Fleet engineering did such a fine job of recruiting young men and women of high technical competence, he thought bitterly. Why couldn't they manage to send him some who were also quick on their feet in the nontechnical aspects?

The younger man was obviously not reassured. "Yes, but sir—"

"Damn it, laddie," Scott said, the anger in his voice quite real and based on his fear for the young man's life. "I know that's not good engineering practice, but we just don't have a choice. Now, don't you mess around with what I've done in there. It's all just on the verge of not holding together, and I don't want you sticking your mitts in there and spoiling what little I was able to do."

The other engineer looked hurt, but he said only, "Yes, sir," and passed on, sedulously checking things off on his clipboard. Scott couldn't tell if he had at last got the message that all was not what it should be or if he had been browbeaten into silence. Either way, he had escaped a brutal death that had been, for some minutes, closer than he could have realized.

The Assassin grasped Scott's upper arm in a grip of

iron. Scott kept the pain from showing. The Assassin stared down into his face for a long moment, perplexity mixed with anger in his expression. Whatever he might suspect, his suspicions were clearly not precise enough for him to act on them. At last he shoved Scott toward the doorway and growled, "Back to the bridge. Move."

Scott moved, releasing the breath he had been unconsciously holding. He knew how close to death *he* had been, but he told himself with some smugness that it had been worth the risk: in the end, the chance he had taken might entirely save his beloved engines and ship from this gang. Suppressing the cocky grin that kept trying to break out on his face, he headed for the elevator.

It could have been called a data exchange, but that does not convey the deeper interchange that was taking place. Christine Chapel sat quietly in a chair in Medical Section, her eyes closed, looking as though she were napping briefly to recover from the rush of wounded. A meter or two away from her, also unmoving, the Onctiliian rested on the floor. Now it was a three-part creature; the once-gaping wound of the dead member was healing rapidly. The three and the new fourth member were reliving each others' lives.

Simultaneously puzzled and entranced, the three Onctiliians experienced Chapel's upbringing on Earth, her academic career, her early professional triumphs, and then the personal loss that had led her to become a nurse in Star Fleet. They ached and wept with her when she found the lover she had thought lost, only to discover that he was even more irretrievably lost than she had known. They comforted her, supported her, wept with her, loved her.

And she lived their childhoods in the marshes of Onctiliis, growing through the many stages of life of that watery world's highest life form. Each life story was repeated three times, though each time differed from the others in some details. Hauntingly, through the memories of the three survivors, she lived the life of the fourth, the one who had died but would never be forgotten or fully relinquished. She relived their meeting in the fern forest that was their tribal mating ground, and then she relived their inexpressibly joyous physical union into a four-part adult. Finally, with them, she lived through their discovery of interplanetary politics, the United Expansion Party, and Hander Morl and his small party of fanatics, and the near-fatal trauma of the death of a member.

Each member contributed something to the personality of the whole. The one who had died had been the most aggressive of the four, and the one most given to sudden and extreme enthusiasms. The being which now included Christine Chapel was not only more intelligent than any other four-part Onctiliian, because the human woman was far more intelligent than any single Onctiliian, but was also more introspective and pacifist. This creature would not have followed Hander Morl. Its memories of what had happened, and the part it had played, horrified the being it had become.

We must correct this evil.

We shall act.

The woman stood up and moved slowly, almost dreamily, from Medical Section into the corridor beyond. The other three, no longer quite able to attain sphericity and thus moving more slowly than normally, followed. The four-part view of the hallway and the four-part body of sensations of smell, sound, and vibrations were a revelation to the member that still called itself "Chapel." It strolled along the corridor, absorbed, delighted, reveling in the profound complexity of the *Enterprise*.

Hander Morl laughed with pleasure as the stars on the main screen dissolved into chaos and then reformed, but this time in evident motion. The *Enterprise*

117

was once more under warp drive, and once again his race toward destiny was on schedule. He pushed himself from the command chair and stretched his cramped muscles, then turned around to grin at Scott, who stood calm and relaxed on the raised platform where Uhura's communications station was located. "Thank you, Chief Engineer. The ship feels good. We're going to make it."

Scott inclined his head slightly but said nothing. Uhura, both puzzled and angry at Scott's complicity with their captors, said, "Thank you indeed, Mr. Scott. That was just what they needed."

In a voice scarcely above a murmur, Scott said, "Don't thank me yet, lass. The best is yet to be."

Chapter Fourteen

The office in which they had spoken to the Klingon was in an underwater dome housing a series of such rooms. As they were led along a succession of corridors under guard, Kirk saw many other such rooms, and they were passed by many Klingons, both singly and in groups. The dome was surely not necessary for the aquatic Sealons. Clearly it had been built only for the sake of their Klingon "advisers," and just as clearly the number of those "advisers" must be very large. The air in the dome was heavy with moisture, and the temperature was too low for human comfort. Water beaded on the walls and dripped from the ceilings. In places, the prisoners and their guards walked through puddles. It was surely well within the abilities of the Klingons to build a more pleasant underwater habitat than this. Kirk assumed that they must see this as only temporary; before too long, they planned to be established on the land and to rule this world, through their Sealon allies, from the surface.

At last they were led to an airlock. Beyond it, they found themselves in a long, pressurized, flexible tube laid on the sea bottom. The tube was well lighted and the walls were partially transparent. As they were marched along it, Kirk could see various sea creatures, shaped much like the fish and sea snakes of his native Earth, nuzzling the outside of the tube, drawn there by the smaller animals that clung to it because of the escaping light and warmth. Under any other circumstances, it would have been a fascinating place to spend some time sightseeing. As it was, he and Spock were hurried along to the end of the tube.

The end was another airlock, on the other side of which they found themselves in a small shuttle craft. The cabin had only one window, small and reinforced to withstand more than normal atmospheric pressure. Kirk and Spock were seated away from the window and manacled to the arms of their acceleration couches. So the Klingons haven't given the Sealons transporters, Kirk thought. Insufficient trust, for true allies, or perhaps it's insufficient faith in their dependability in the future.

Noises came from beyond the airlock, and then the shuttle was free and rising up through the sea. Startled shapes moved beyond the window, sea creatures disturbed by the sudden motion of their new habitat. Once, something large swam up and a face that looked like a cross between a man's and a frog's stared in at them. A Sealon, Kirk realized, either a curious one or a suspicious one, checking up on the latest movements of the Klingons. The Klingon guard seated by the window recoiled in open disgust and put his hand reflexively to his phaser. Then the Sealon face disappeared. Kirk glanced at Spock and saw that the Vulcan was watching the Klingon with the same interest he felt.

The shuttle broke the surface and lay bobbing for a few minutes on the swells in bright sunlight. The window showed alternations of bright blue sky and green waters as the waves broke against the vessel's side. Then there was the rumble of engines and, sluggishly at first, the shuttle raised itself into the air. Gathering speed, it flashed upwards at a steep angle, the blue sky outside the window giving place to a deeper, darker color and then finally to the star-speckled black of space. This was a rare experience for Kirk, who was accustomed to using the *Enterprise*'s transporter and could only rarely allow himself the luxury of traveling by shuttle. Time was usually so short for his many duties that he normally considered the shuttle as much an inconvenience as a luxury. Now, with no choice in the matter, he could revel in the sense of community the experience gave him with the first men to leave the Earth atop their chemical rockets and thrust into space. James Kirk had few heroes, but those men were among them. Then the craft turned slightly and beyond the window part of a Klingon-inspired Sealon ship came into view, and Kirk's fantasies evaporated.

The manacles were unlocked, Kirk and Spock were transferred to the large ship quickly and efficiently and placed in a detention cell, and the ship left orbit for Sealon. Except for the Sealons who had captured them on the beach and the enigmatic face at the shuttle's window while it was still underwater, Kirk had seen only Klingons. He began to wonder if the Klingons had already followed their usual pattern of reducing their vassal peoples to slavery, without even waiting for the invasion of Trellisane to be completed. Were there even any Sealons aboard this apparently Sealon ship? He filed the anomaly away for future reference, along with the reaction of the Klingon guard to the face at the shuttle's window, not knowing yet what use any of this information might be but hoping that it would be of some use in the future. If I have a future, he reminded himself.

Veedron had heard enough. He leaped from his chair and stalked to the door of McCoy's office. He paused there, turned his head, and said to the doctor, "I had no idea your Federation had such stupid laws. We'll certainly have to reconsider any idea of joining it.

You'd expect us to share political power with the *yegemot*—creatures whose ancestors weren't even human!" Head high with anger, he started to leave the room.

McCoy stared speechlessly at him for a moment, then called him back before he was out of earshot. "Veedron! Wait just a minute. What was that last thing you said?"

Veedron came back into the office reluctantly and seated himself again. "The *yegemot,* those with no *gemot.* That's what we call them, the ones you call our servants. I haven't explained this to you before because we don't talk about it to outsiders when they come here to trade. We try to spare the *yegemot* the embarrassment. After all, even they have some feelings, almost as we do."

"Oh, I'm sure that's true," McCoy said, but his irony was apparently lost on Veedron.

"Yes," Veedron said, "they do, although not everyone seems to realize that. You see, McCoy, the *yegemot* are actually descended from domestic animals that our ancestors bred to human shape ages ago. Unfortunately, that sort of biological skill has been long lost to us, but fortunately the *yegemot* breed true. I'd be the first to admit that our economy depends upon continuing their breed. There's never a shortage of them." He sniffed in contempt. "I suppose that's one advantage of their lack of a moral code. Now, I know that you have various animals as pets and for some work on Earth. Would you ever consider letting them vote or share in the running of your world? Of course not! And yet that is just what you expect us to do here on Trellisane."

"Then a . . . *yegemot* may achieve as high a level of competence in some field or profession as possible and still not be accepted as one of you?"

"Of course not. Anyway, they are not mentally capable of reaching a very high level of competence in anything."

"Because they're really animals in human guise?"

"Precisely!" Veedron was triumphant. "There, McCoy, now you begin to understand. Now perhaps you can sympathize with our point of view."

"Veedron, I'm probably better equipped to understand your attitude than anyone else on the *Enterprise.* Tell me, though. Has it ever happened that a *yegemot* has, um, mated with a human and produced young?"

Veedron stiffened in anger. As McCoy had anticipated, this was a question that struck a bit too deep for comfort. Then the Trellisanian relaxed again and said, slowly, as if each word were being dragged from him painfully, "Yes. It has happened. Our deepest shame. Such children are considered to be *yegemot* themselves."

McCoy put his hands behind his head and leaned back in his chair, looking thoughtfully at the ceiling. "Your ancestors must have been smarter than you realize. They've made biological history here."

Veedron smiled, his anger forgotten. "I'm so glad that you, at least, understand our position."

"Oh, I do indeed," McCoy said. "This does change matters in some respects."

Veedron left the office again, but this time not in anger. There was a bounce in his step. McCoy watched him go thoughtfully, then got up and followed him.

They were brought down from orbit by shuttle craft again. The vessel landed on a strip on a small land mass that Kirk, searching his memory for the few details Veedron had told them when they arrived on Trellisane, guessed must be the land capital built by Pongol, the great leader who had united Sealon. The land was covered with huge buildings, topped by tall chimneys from which black smoke belched. Land and air traffic moved about busily. Nature had forced the Sealons to build all of this on land, no matter how much their own biology might make them prefer the sea.

A Klingon guard—again, no sign of Sealons—marched them from the shuttle to a small surface craft. In that they were taken to a large office building, much like an administrative center on any planet. The grounds and the corridors of this building bustled with Klingons, striding about with evident purpose.

They were taken to a large, grand office in the building. A Klingon officer, his high rank indicated by the braid on his uniform, waited behind a large desk for them. As their guard ushered them in, he rose and greeted them in a surprising display of politeness. He was tall, broad, heavily muscled—huge for a Klingon, and gigantic by Earth standards. He wore the short, well-trimmed beard common among Klingon officers; his skin color was even darker than most. He radiated power, confidence, and an unstoppable will. His voice matched that impression—deep, resonant, powerful. He spoke quietly, almost gently, for a Klingon. "Captain Kirk and Mr. Spock. I am Fleet Leader Kaged, commandant of all Klingon forces in this system. I am quite pleased to meet both of you after all these years."

"Quite pleased to have us captive, you mean," Kirk said.

Kaged inclined his head slightly. "Of course that. But in addition, I'm pleased to meet you in person. I've followed your career with interest and admiration, Captain. There is surely no other officer in Star Fleet who has performed so well against us. Therefore, I am pleased to have you captive and no longer able to act against us; but I am also glad to have the chance to speak to you."

This reception threw Kirk momentarily off balance. To keep that from showing, he said, "You know the situation with my ship. There won't be any time for talk if the Romulans arrive here and attack your installation. You don't know them as we do, Kaged. They're capable of just such a response."

Kaged laughed suddenly, a loud, booming laugh with

an undertone of cruelty and threat—the true Klingon in him peeping out from behind the mask of politeness. "We don't fear the Romulans, Kirk, any more than we fear the Federation. They worry more about fighting honorably than about winning. Fortunately, we aren't hampered that way." He pursed his lips in momentary thought. "Still, it would be inconvenient to have to deal with them now, before we're ready. They're on our schedule, you know," he said, suddenly conversational and polite again, "but the Federation comes first."

He's talking too much, Kirk realized suddenly. He wouldn't say all of this to us if he expected to ever let us go. Somehow, Kirk had always thought he'd die in battle, as a warrior, not that he'd be coldbloodedly executed while a prisoner of the Klingons. "The more you talk, the closer the *Enterprise* gets to the Neutral Zone."

Kaged nodded. "Preparations are already underway. After this problem is solved, I must extract from you the story of your loss of the *Enterprise*. Captain Kirk, of all men—our great nemesis. You've destroyed so many Klingon vessels, you and your ship. To have you lose your own to an attack from the inside—why, it astonishes me!"

Kirk gritted his teeth but said nothing. Kaged watched him carefully for signs of some response, but Kirk's control of his expression was firm enough that the Klingon looked away finally, disappointed. "Yes," Kaged said. After a pause, he continued, "I'm going to give you something you've probably long desired, Kirk: a ride on a first-line Klingon battleship. I'm sure you'd prefer to be in command of her, having captured her in battle, but you'll have to settle for being a prisoner."

"What do you have in mind, Kaged?"

"Unfortunately, I have only a small fleet here at my command, and I'm reluctant to divide it. I've decided to send the largest ship off after the *Enterprise*. Its speed is greater than anything the Federation has, so it should be able to catch the *Enterprise* before it reaches Romulan territory. The new higher speed we've been able to attain is something I wouldn't normally want you to know about until you met us in battle, but," he shrugged his shoulders and smirked, "in your case it hardly matters what you find out. You'll be on the ship as an expert adviser to its captain. After all, who knows more about the *Enterprise* and its crew and capabilities —and how to find, fight, and destroy her—than the great Captain James T. Kirk?"

"You expect me to help you destroy my own ship?" Kirk was as amazed as he was angry.

Kaged looked at him shrewdly. "I don't think your Federation is any readier to fight the Romulans than we are, Kirk. We watched you carefully when the Romulans first attacked you. You gave back, nearly collapsed. You just barely managed to hold your own against them. Had we only been ready at the time to take advantage of it, we could have mopped you up afterwards in no time. Since then, we believe, the Federation has grown even more pacifist and weaker, while the Romulans, hidden behind their Neutral Zone —well, who knows what time and resentment might have done for them? Kirk, I respect you personally, even admire you, as many Klingon military commanders do. If you were typical of Star Fleet ship's captains, it would be a different situation. As it is, your Federation is doomed as soon as we Klingons can find some way around the Organians and attack you. That might take generations, however; certainly, the Federation should survive during your lifetime and mine. Unless you go to war with the Romulans, of course, in which case they will probably wipe you out before we have the chance to do so. It's your ship, your *Enterprise,* against the survival of the Federation. I'm offering you the chance to save the Federation by helping us."

In the meantime weakening the Federation by the

loss of the finest ship and crew in the fleet, Kirk thought bitterly.

Spock said, "On the face of it, Captain, a logical argument."

"On the face of it!" Kaged exclaimed. "Logical all the way through, Vulcan. Moreover, you will stay behind with me. Kirk, to ensure that you won't try one of your famous stratagems, Spock remains here as a hostage. I think we could manage to make even a Vulcan feel a great deal of pain before he died, despite their mental disciplines."

"An interesting challenge, sir," Spock said thoughtfully. "I shall be most curious to see whether your methods of torture are indeed so efficacious as you seem to think."

Kirk shuddered involuntarily at the thought and at Spock's coldblooded discussion of his own fate. "It won't come to that, Mr. Spock," he said quietly, wearily. "I agree, Kaged." He came closer in that moment to admitting total defeat than he had ever done in his career.

The quiet, small sounds of utensils against plates, the gentle tinkling of glasses being filled with exquisite wines, the low murmur of civilized conversation. Half a dozen men were present at the banquet, besides Leonard McCoy; they were the ones who had happened to be on this continent when the Sealons cut off transoceanic travel. Still, they were the leaders of most of this world's most powerful and important *gemots,* and thus, sitting in council, they were what government Trellisane had. McCoy was an honored guest, and in fact he was being treated by these powerful leaders as one of them.

The food was exclusively vegetarian. This puzzled McCoy and annoyed him somewhat. The fish he had had before was missing. Well, of course, no fisherman in his right mind would go out on the sea, with the current conditions, and on this world, fresh-water fish weren't considered sufficient delicacies to be served in such elevated company. The marine plants the Trellisanians ate—and which McCoy was already learning to detest, after eating them three times a day every day—had previously been harvested on the high seas but were now being grown on shallow bays and inland salt pools. But what he particularly missed was the meat he had been fed upon arrival. He longed to sink his teeth into a juicy, medium-rare steak. That stuff was raised on land, of course, so what was the problem? Or have they, he wondered, killed off all the herds already in panic over coming shortages? He turned to his neighbor on his right, a distinguished, elderly, grey-bearded gentleman wearing the subdued robes of the Building Erectors *gemot*. "You know," McCoy said to him in a low voice, "I wouldn't mind some food with a lot less crunch and a lot more blood in it."

His neighbor nodded and murmured, "Indeed. I'm quite shocked that, with a guest such as you present, proper food was not provided. I must have a word with Geldop about this."

"Who?"

"Ah, of course, you wouldn't know. Geldop is the current head of the Food Provenders' *gemot*." He raised himself slightly in his chair and looked around. Then he sighed heavily. "I see he is not with us. Perhaps he was trapped elsewhere by the war, or possibly even injured or killed, poor man. Still," he said, looking righteous again, "that *gemot* has many able men in lower positions, and this laxity is inexcusable." He gestured over his shoulder at the line of quiet waiters standing against the wall behind them. "Just feast your eyes on that row of healthy, young *yegemot*. Truly shocking."

McCoy bridled. "Well, now—" But at this point, he

was interrupted by the beginning of a speech, and by the time it was over, he had lost his train of thought.

Later, as he was leaving the banquet hall, satisfied with the drink if not with the food, McCoy encountered Spenreed strolling down the hallway, looking jubilant. "Doctor!" the *yegemot* burst out, grabbing his hand. "I was hoping to find you here. I don't know what you did to me when you operated on me, but I think you saved my life twice. I'm still alive!"

"I've noticed you are," McCoy said, extracting his hand from the slave's powerful grip. Flexing his hand, he added, "But it wasn't anything I did. Don't you see, it was just some foolish superstitious idea you had, and as I told you, those are nonsense no matter what planet you're on."

Spenreed laughed joyfully. "Oh, yes, Doctor. It's all nonsense, all right. You've changed my attitudes about a lot of things." He walked on down the hallway, whistling, with a bounce in his step. McCoy grinned after him, shook his head, and went about his own business.

Chapter Fifteen

Honorable warriors they might be, but the Romulans were not above monitoring Federation communications from within the Neutral Zone. They had caught even less of the message from Trellisane than had been recorded by the colony on Trefolg, so they had no idea the Klingons were in any way involved. Nonetheless, a war within the no-man's-land, in a system not too far removed from their own borders, and an appeal for help to the Federation disturbed them mightily. Patrols in the general direction of Trellisane were increased both in number and strength, special bases were established to listen for more messages, and military forces in the area were ordered to be even more alert than usual. If a patrol should occasionally, overcome with zeal and devotion to duty, stray beyond the Neutral Zone in order to patrol more effectively, no one was reprimanded. There were powerful factions within the Romulan military command and high imperial circles who were eager to renew the war with the Federation.

Sulu watched the four points on his screen for long moments, wondering whether patriotism would be better served by speaking out or remaining silent. At last, loyalty to his ship won out over other questions and he said, "Something's headed our way." There was no response from the command chair, where Hander Morl was staring at him uncomprehendingly. "I'll put it on the main screen," Sulu said, hiding his sneer with only partial success.

The starfield on the main screen wavered and dissolved and was replaced with a view that at first glance seemed similar. However, near the center of the image, four bright points moved together against the background stars. Sulu looked over his shoulder quickly at Morl, but the man who should have been issuing commands was staring at the screen in obvious puzzlement. "Ships, probably," Sulu said, open contempt in his voice. "I'll magnify." Again the image wavered, dissolved, then resolidified. This time, the dots took shape as four strangely shaped warships, growing steadily larger as they sped toward the *Enterprise*. Sulu felt a prickling at the back of his neck. "Romulans," he whispered. In the sudden, tense silence on the bridge, the whisper carried to every corner.

Hander Morl sat frozen, his eyes bulging. Earlier, he had reveled in the feeling of being in control of this great weapon, at the nerve center of this embodiment of Federation might. He had looked forward to the final confrontation with the Romulans, the moment that would both end and epitomize his career. Now that moment was here, and he was suddenly paralyzed with fear. Those ships, those fiendish, evil shapes rushing down on them! How could they survive? How could they escape? He looked around the bridge. The *Enterprise* personnel were concentrating on their instruments, sparing only an occasional glance at the screen, and Morl was overcome by a wave of admiration for their courage and sense of duty. His own people were watching him for a cue. "Have we reached the Neutral Zone yet?" he tried to ask Sulu, but his voice came out as an incoherent croak. He cleared his throat and repeated the question, this time intelligibly.

"No." It was Chekov who answered him. "We're

some distance from it yet. Those ships penetrated beyond it."

Morl felt relief and triumph. "Then they've already precipitated the war by violating our space!"

Scott, still standing calmly next to Uhura, said, "I doubt it. This area wasn't covered in the treaty. It's outside both our space and theirs."

"Then we can't fight them here!" Morl said desperately. "We've got to reach the Neutral Zone first. Increase our speed!"

Sulu shook his head. "Sorry. We'll need the screens up if they're chasing and firing at us, and that means no more speed than we already have." He doubted if Morl would know better.

"I'm getting something," Uhura said. "They want us to kill the warp drive and stand by for boarding. They want to know what we're doing here."

"Boarding!" Morl went pale. If he allowed the ship to be boarded and captured, that would be the certain end of all his plans. "All right. Kill the warp immediately." Sulu and Chekov exchanged a glance of triumph, thinking that Morl was defeated at last; their pleasure kept them from noticing the sudden determination in his voice. Sulu's fingers moved over the buttons of his console and, with that psychophysical wrench, the *Enterprise* dropped back into normal space.

"Speed at zero," Sulu said happily. It would be more honorable to be taken prisoner by the Romulans, he reflected, than to be part of a plot to cause a war.

While Sulu, Chekov, and the others turned from their work to watch the Romulan ships approach ever closer on the main screen, Morl asked Scott, "How will they board us?"

Scott shrugged. "Hard to say. They might use a shuttle, or they might decide to beam directly onto the bridge."

Morl nodded in satisfaction. He pushed himself from

the chair and strode energetically over to Sulu's chair. "Out," he said. "Quickly."

Sulu laughed but stood up. Morl sat down in his place. Sulu grinned at his back and said, "Don't touch anything, kid."

But Morl ignored him. His fingers moved carefully but rapidly over the buttons of the helmsman's console. He had spent months studying the blueprints and operating manuals for such starships as this one, and he had spent the last many weary hours carefully watching Sulu's actions. This and his intelligence stood him in good stead now. Sulu, watching him, lost his grin and felt instead grudging but genuine admiration. Morl finished composing the series of commands, checked them quickly on the small screen on the console, and then stopped with his finger over the button that would start the execution of the commands. With everyone else, he watched the Romulan ships in the main screen.

The four ships were arranged as the vertices of an almost precise square. They retained that formation, approaching and slowing until the *Enterprise* was at the center of the square. There they stopped. The tension of waiting increased. Nothing further seemed to be happening. Scott stepped quickly to the science officer station and pressed his face to the visor of the small computer console. "They're scanning the bridge now," he announced. "Probably trying to establish coordinates for their transporter. Yes, here it comes."

Simultaneously, half a dozen vaguely manlike shapes began to resolve themselves on the *Enterprise* bridge in the display of twinkling lights characteristic of a transporter, and Morl pressed the button on the console firmly. There was a sudden jolt of impulse power and the six shapes, fixed in space, seemed to move sideways sharply and out through the walls of the bridge into space as the *Enterprise* moved away from them. Almost immediately, the warp engines cut in and the Romulan ships on the screen disappeared. Morl grinned at Sulu, who, struck with horror at this callousness and imagining himself in the position of the Romulans in the transporter beam, yelled at Chekov, "Get that on the screen! Full magnification!"

Chekov fumbled with his console for a moment, then succeeded. The scene was shrinking rapidly as the *Enterprise* sped away, but even so Sulu could make out the six shapes in airless space, writhing and struggling as they suffocated and their tissues ruptured. Just as they were lost in the distance, he thought they twinkled out of sight, brought back aboard their ships by transporter, but he knew it was probably too late to save their lives. For a Romulan above all, he thought, that must have seemed a filthy, evil death, killed by trickery and dishonesty. And cruelly and uncleanly. The Romulans would not let them go now.

Morl stood up and returned to the command chair, a spring in his step. "That's how to do it!" he said, not trying to hide his pleasure. "That's how a patriot takes care of those animals. Now, get the screens up if they get close enough to fire. Otherwise, just keep us ahead of them until we can penetrate their home space."

Sulu returned to his position, feeling ill. He raged at himself. Wasn't there something they could do against this madman, despite his underlings and their weapons? For the first time that he could remember, he felt more kinship with the Romulans than with his own kind.

Unity through diversity. That is the philosophy of the unit called Spock. Spock: the new union had not destroyed old emotions. Nor were feelings hidden from the new partners, even if those feelings had once been partially, unsuccessfully hidden from herself. The wave of feeling ran from the human body to the other three and rebounded. But with it came warm support and commiseration, sympathy and empathy for unrequited love.

A good philosophy. It describes our union and its beauty.

It is what Hander Morl and the others do not see—what we did not see, before . . . before . . .

Before the death of the original fourth member. This time, it was the human partner who supported and soothed the others, calming the panic-hurt of the terrible wound.

Therefore the United Expansion Party must be stopped. Hander Morl and his followers must be shown their error and persuaded to halt.

The being moved toward a turboelevator, waited until the doors swished open, and then stepped inside. The process happened twice, for the being had two bodies, and one of those was in three parts and moved with difficulty. A momentary pause, while the memories of the human member were searched and she—Chapel to herself, still, but less so with every passing minute—struggled to speak. "Bridge."

"Bridge has been ordered closed to all personnel not already working there." The voice was almost apologetic.

Again the memories were searched. "Medical emergency. This is Nurse Christine Chapel. Check my voice pattern and comply with my first command."

The pause was long, as if the computer, presented by a second demand to override its command from the bridge on the basis of an emergency, had grown suspicious. The voice pattern did not match precisely that in its files for Chapel, but the deviation was within the allowable amount, despite its strangeness, and it had no choice but to comply. Had the bridge foreseen this, it would have commanded the computer to notify it of any override, but Morl had not thought of that.

As the elevator began to move, the ship's warp drive cut off once more, and the *Enterprise* dropped back into normal space. The effect was insignificant to the machines onboard, and even to most humans; once they had had a chance to grow used to it, the wrench of transition, more psychological than physical, was only a minor nuisance. To the new being in the elevator, however, the transition was a shattering blow. The transition took place when the elevator was passing through a region of the ship where the shielding against its effects was inadequate. The wrenching effect would have been much greater than normal for any other being, but still bearable. Not so for this four-part creature.

Chapel crumpled to the floor nervelessly and lay there unmoving and unthinking for long minutes. The other three cried out in pain as she fell and then grew silent, watching her in confusion. Shakily, bewildered, she rose to her feet.

Who is this strange human with us?

A threat!

Shall we kill it?

She stared back at them, filled with an unutterable loss. Contact had been broken, communion lost. She remembered her previous state, but they, reeling from their earlier losses, their subsequent brush with death, and the new union with so alien a mind as Chapel's, scarcely remembered her. She felt their intentions and pressed herself against the farther wall in fear. They poised themselves for an attack.

And then the elevator passed into a well shielded area and even the transitory effects still remaining from the transition to normal space vanished. Slowly a trickle of telepathic contact began, growing quickly to a rush, a flood of sensation and memory, and the four minds rushed together again into the communion with a cry of gladness both physical and mental. The merger was deeper than ever. Chapel and the others knew with even greater keenness than before what they had gained and how fragile it was.

* * *

Hander Morl raged futilely as he paced about the bridge. "You!" he screamed, pointing at Scott. His finger and his voice both shook, but he was beyond noticing either. "Why did this happen?" He had ordered Sulu to demand warp speed again from Engineering section, but the reply from below had been that the warp reactor had stopped and could not be restarted. Morl knew what Scott would reply—that he had warned Morl this would happen if he was not allowed to replace those mysterious parts in the reactor—and he could even guess at the smugness of Scott's smile as he gave this answer. Therefore he gave Scott no chance to answer. "Never mind. Just get back down there and fix it as soon as possible." As Scott headed for the elevator doors, Hander Morl motioned quickly at one of his Assassin bodyguards to follow the engineer. But even as he did so, he wondered why he was bothering. Did it make any difference now? He had a sinking feeling in the pit of his stomach. *Something:* there must still be something he could do, even now.

The Romulans had been caught by surprise by the shift from warp drive and had overshot the *Enterprise,* but not by much. Now they too had returned to normal space and were heading swiftly back toward their prey. "Full power to shields," Sulu ordered calmly, filled with that icy coolness that overcomes some men in battle, all the more so when they are sure they will not live through it. With so little room or power to maneuver, the *Enterprise* must either surrender or face the concentrated fire of the four Romulan ships. Her shields would not hold up for long under such a bombardment. Perhaps there would have been a chance with a superb tactician like Captain Kirk in command, Sulu thought. He had pulled them out of even worse situations before. But with this madman in control, either surrender or death was inevitable.

The small display above the elevator doors indicated that another elevator had arrived and was queued, waiting its turn, waiting for Scott to leave for Engineering in the elevator already there. Scott noted that fact with some surprise and then noted that no one else was aware of it. It might be help on its way, he told himself. In that case, I can do much more good up here on the bridge than down in Engineering.

The doors had not yet opened, since Scott had not yet stepped within range of the sensors. He turned to the Assassin walking close beside him and said conversationally, "Sometimes you have to keep reminding these elevators that you want them, or else the computer forgets about you." He stepped to the side and pressed the array of buttons beside the elevator doors quickly, appearing to be summoning an elevator. In fact, he had issued an override command, ordering the computer to dispatch the waiting car elsewhere and instead allow the queued one to come up to the doors. Then he stepped back to his previous position, trying to look calm, but burning with hope.

"Here they come," Sulu muttered. The four Romulan ships swept down upon the *Enterprise* and matched trajectories with her. The Federation ship was at the center of the square, with a Romulan at each corner.

"They demand surrender," Uhura said.

Hander Morl gritted his teeth. "No!" he hissed. "Fight the animals!"

Sitting ducks, Sulu thought. That's what we are. Aloud, he said, "Arm photon torpedoes."

Chapter Sixteen

It had been a few days since McCoy had had the opportunity to remove a capsule from the brain of a slave. Now he had just done it again, and after closing the patient's skull, he stepped over to the shelf where he had been keeping the capsules removed previously to add the new one to the collection. To keep them from rolling away, he had put the lot of them in a bowl. Now, bowl and capsules were gone, and so was part of the shelf. Where the bowl had stood was a hole in the shelf. The wood had been burned through in an almost perfectly circular pattern, with charred edges bearing mute witness to the heat required. He bent down to examine the underside of the shelf above, and it too was blackened, although it still seemed strong enough to hold the beakers he had placed on it. Below the hole, on the next shelf down, he had put replacement units for the hypospray charge. Some of these, directly beneath the hole, had melted, spilling their contents across the shelf. The others were discolored, the fluids in them opaque. McCoy cursed. "Spenreed!"

The slave had attached himself to McCoy as permanent assistant, assuring the Earthman that he would no longer be needed at his previous place. Now he came running. "Look at this mess!" McCoy said. "These hypospray units are worthless now. Throw them out and see if I have any more in the stuff I brought down with me from the *Enterprise*. Do you have any idea what happened here?" He pointed at the hole in the shelf.

Spenreed shook his head, looking mystified.

"All right, all right. Get going." As the slave hurried from the room, the bundle of ruined hypospray units clutched in his arms, McCoy muttered, "I wonder if there was something funny about that bowl. . . ."

There was a crash from the next room, and a bellow in a voice McCoy recognized as Veedron's. "Animal!" Veedron shouted. "How dare you!"

McCoy ran in to find the two Trellisanians facing each other, both red faced. The hypospray units littered the floor. "Animal yourself!" Spenreed shouted. "You think the world belongs to you, your kind! Watch your step next time."

Veedron's eyes widened in disbelief. Then stern anger ruled his face. He pointed at the slave and closed his eyes, his expression becoming one of deep inner concentration.

Spenreed sank back against a wall, collapsing to the floor, his hands over his face, and moaned. His impertinence had vanished, and he was white and trembling in terror.

And nothing happened.

Veedron opened his eyes and said smugly, "There!" Then he saw Spenreed rising to his feet again. Now it was the aristocrat's turn to pale with fear. "Oh, no!" Veedron muttered. He ran from the room.

Spenreed's cockiness returned as quickly as it had left him. His voice, though, was still shaky when he said, "I think you've saved me three times now, Doctor! I've got to tell others about this." He skipped from the room.

It can't be, McCoy said to himself. It just can't be what I think it is. My God, what kind of a world is this?

The Klingon ship was huge, perhaps three times the size of the *Enterprise.* The bridge was considerably more than three times as big as the *Enterprise*'s bridge, and thus seemingly out of all proportion to the size of the ship. During his long, weary hours there under guard, Kirk realized why this was so. The operation of this monster vessel was apparently divided into sections, just as a Federation starship, but the emphasis was different. The Klingons' Medical section was tiny: the Klingon Empire preferred not to expend its resources on the ill or wounded, with the inevitable exception of the upper-level officer cadre. Security, on the other hand, was enormous, representing, Kirk guessed, about half the ship's personnel. This was so, simply enough, because everyone was under almost constant surveillance—even the Security personnel themselves.

The center for this operation was not in some distant, removed area of the ship, but rather right on the bridge. That way, the ship's captain could keep his own eye on the Security men. One whole side of the bridge, almost half the available area, was given over to these men, sitting patiently and quietly before their banks of miniature screens, watching ship's personnel throughout the vessel and listening to their conversations. Who was watching the captain? Kirk wondered. He remembered being told by the Klingon Commander Kor on Organia that every Klingon official was always under careful scrutiny, every action and word watched and weighed. Perhaps someone, somewhere, in some hidden cubicle, was watching the bridge, the captain, and Kirk at that very moment, ready to report instantly to his superiors on Sealon if he saw or heard anything smacking of treason or weakness.

One thing at least was on a smaller scale than its equivalent on the *Enterprise,* and that was the main viewing screen on the bridge. Had this been the bridge of a Federation ship, with the main screen showing as bizarre a sight as this one, everyone on the bridge would have been watching it. Klingon crews were much more strictly disciplined; on this bridge, only Kirk and Karox, the Klingon captain, were watching the screen.

Five points of light were displayed there, moving at sublight speed against the background of stars. Four of them were arranged in a square, with the fifth at its center. Karox called out, "Full magnification!" But even before his order was implemented, Kirk knew what he would see. The magnified picture verified his premonition and sent a chill through him. He scarcely heard Karox's next order, to kill the warp drive and maintain present distance from the action depicted on the screen.

There in miniature was the *Enterprise,* under attack by four Romulan vessels. All five ships were surrounded by the haze of defensive screens. Even as they watched, twin photon torpedoes, visible as two brilliant points of light, streaked from the *Enterprise* toward one corner of the square. One torpedo missed, continuing off the screen, but the other hit, and the hazy glow of the Romulan's shield flickered and momentarily died. The *Enterprise* followed with a quick barrage of phaser fire. The defenseless Romulan ship flared up in a bright, explosive glow and then vanished.

Karox pounded his fist on the arm of his command chair and shouted, "Good shot, Kirk! Well done! You're better fighters than I thought." He sat back in his chair and said, more calmly, "But the end is inevitable. The Romulans won't let that happen again. Your ship is doomed."

Kirk knew he was right. The glow around the surviving Romulans brightened as they increased their shield power. They began a steady phaser attack on the

Enterprise; even with their phasers' power reduced because of their increased screening, the total effect was still enormous. The glow of the *Enterprise*'s own screens slowly faded as the ship's energy reserves dwindled. The Federation ship fired off her remaining photon torpedoes, but the increased screens of the Romulans protected them from serious damage, and the *Enterprise* didn't try any more phaser attacks, since to have taken any more power from her screens would only have hastened the inevitable.

"Something must be wrong with her warp engines," Karox muttered, "or she'd get herself out of there." His interest was obvious, but he was detached. The scene that wrenched Kirk so was to the Klingon merely an impersonal tactical problem.

Kirk was manacled to the arms of his chair, set firmly into the floor near Karox's. He ached to do something for his ship, but he was heavily guarded and could not have made a move even if he could somehow have removed the metal bands around his wrists. "Karox," he said hoarsely. "You've got to do something to stop it. You were ordered to keep the *Enterprise* and the Romulans apart. This is a powerful ship. Attack the Romulans!"

Karox laughed at him, enjoying the distress Kirk could no longer hide. "We're not ready for that war quite yet, Captain Kirk. We're not going to fight the Federation's wars for it! We attack only when we feel prepared." He paused for a moment, thinking over his words. "My orders were only to catch up with the *Enterprise* and destroy it. It appears that the Romulans are going to do that job for me, so that my ship will remain unharmed. It occurs to me that we are not yet within the Romulan Neutral Zone. I'm not sure of the ramifications of the Romulans being out here, beyond the Neutral Zone, and attacking a Federation ship, but in any case we're too late to prevent that from happening. If the Romulans destroy the *Enterprise* without boarding her, as I think they're about to do, then they won't know where she came from, and there will be no Romulan threat to our operations on Sealon and Trellisane."

"But their suspicions will be aroused," Kirk said desperately. "They might decide to investigate this whole region of space."

"They're even more likely to do that if I attack them and they get word of it back before I can destroy all three of them." Karox leaned toward Kirk and said in a low voice, "Kirk, if Romulan suspicions are aroused, and if it's not my fault, then it will be clear that it's Kaged's fault. He will be removed in disgrace, and I will move up to his position." He sat back, smiling at the thought. "I should have been promoted into that in the first place. No, I think we'll just stay where we are, beyond the sensor range of those four, and watch to the end."

Beyond sensor range, Kirk thought, his military training reasserting itself even in this moment of ultimate despair. That must mean that, in addition to the great ship's enormous speed, which he had already found frighteningly impressive, she could obtain clear visual images at a range that was greater than that of both Federation and Romulan sensors. He knew his higher duty: to survive himself, no matter if his ship was lost, so that he could get word back to Star Fleet of this double Klingon military advantage.

"Now," Karox said, leaning forward toward the screen. The *Enterprise*'s screens had gone down completely, and she was a helpless target. Kirk watched helplessly, wanting to look away but somehow unable to as he waited for the final Romulan attack that would disintegrate his ship.

For what seemed an eternity, nothing happened. Then the Romulan ships rearranged themselves to form an equilateral triangle, still with the *Enterprise* at the center of their formation, and faint yellow lines sprang into being, linking each Romulan ship to each of the other two and to the *Enterprise*. "What is that?" Karox demanded.

One of the bridge personnel inspected the instruments before him and answered his captain. "Some sort of tractor beam, sir. Very unusual characteristics."

Karox glared at the man, then returned his attention to the screen. Suddenly, all four ships vanished. Karox cursed loudly in Klingon. "Warp drive," he muttered. "How did they manage to pull something with the mass of a starship into warp with them? Worthy opponents, those Romulans."

"Karox," Kirk said quickly, "don't you see what they're doing? They're taking my ship back into the Neutral Zone with them, and then they're going to board her and interrogate the crew. They'll find out about Sealon and send a force there. And it *will* be your fault, for letting them take the *Enterprise!*"

Karox looked at him for a moment and then cursed again. "You're right, Kirk, damn you." He barked a string of orders at his helmsman, and the great Klingon warship shot into warp drive in pursuit of the Romulans and their captives.

"Reduce it again," Hander Morl ordered, and Sulu complied reluctantly. With each fresh barrage of phaser fire from the Romulans, he had been ordered to reduce the *Enterprise*'s shield strength. At first, this had seemed to him to be simply further madness. Suddenly he saw the point. The shield would give way eventually anyway, under the combined effect of fire from the three enemy ships. Keeping it at the fullest strength the ship could manage would only buy them a small amount of time. But by reducing the shields steadily, so that it looked to the Romulans as though the shields had already failed, the *Enterprise* would keep something in reserve for possible future action. Sulu's admiration was grudging but genuine.

Sulu reduced the shield strength the last, small step, and the *Enterprise* was defenseless. Damage reports started flooding in, tinny voices in his earphones filled with fear and confusion. Sulu gritted his teeth and ignored them: he could see from the main screen that the phaser fire from the Romulans had already decreased; at last it stopped entirely.

"They're giving us one last chance to surrender," Uhura said.

Morl nodded. "Accept. Tell them we surrender."

The main viewing screen showed the strange beams springing up, linking the Romulans and the starship. There was a small jerk as tractor contact was made.

"Now what?" Chekov said.

Sulu shook his head. "Never seen anything like that before," he muttered. "Tractor beams? What do they want to do that for?"

The transition to warp drive was totally unexpected but unmistakable. "Engineer!" Morl shouted. "I thought it wasn't working!"

Scott's jaw dropped. He stepped forward a few paces, away from the elevator doors, to get a better look at the viewing screen. "By God!" he said. "It's not ours! They've got some way to take us into warp drive with them!"

Hander Morl relaxed, his face breaking into a broad grin. "This is better than I could have hoped. They're taking us into the Neutral Zone, at least, for interrogation, and we still have some shield capability and our phasers. We'll get the battle we came for, after all!"

All attention was riveted on the strange sight on the main viewing screen. Unnoticed by anyone on the bridge, the elevator doors swished open.

Chapter Seventeen

Before the combined stresses of fear and isolation—
held captive on a small island on a hostile world, seeing
no one but Klingons—a human being might have given
way before long. Not so a Vulcan. The Klingons had
Spock's cell under constant surveillance, of course, but
it was they who were giving way before Spock's imper-
turbability. Klingons are an excitable, impatient species
under the best of conditions, and the sight of Spock
sitting on his bunk, staring blankly into space for hour
after hour, his face as impassive as always, drove the
watchers to distraction.

Spock's application of Vulcan mental disciplines was
suddenly broken by a shout and crashing noises from
down the corridor. Spock sprang to the door of his cell,
leaning as close to the dangerous force field as he
dared, to try to see into the hallway. But the archway of
the cell's entrance extended outward too far because of
the thickness of the walls, and he could see nothing.
Now Spock was showing a hint of the impatience and
worry the Klingon watchers had been waiting for;
however, they were now otherwise occupied and could
spare no glances for their spy screens.

There was a succession of unidentifiable sounds—
loud, harsh growls with a shrill overtone—followed by

more crashes. And then the lights in the cell and the corridor went out and Spock found himself in utter blackness. Without even a moment's hesitation, Spock stepped forward. His estimate of the risk was justified by the results: the force field had vanished with the lights.

He walked down the narrow corridor in the pitch black, carefully, his arms out to either side, fingertips trailing along the walls. His finely tuned Vulcan hearing was strained to the utmost, listening for what he could not see. Spock thought it more than likely that a Klingon or two might be walking down the same hallway in the same manner. But not even a Vulcan can calculate odds correctly when important data are missing, and there were factors involved of which Spock as yet knew nothing. He encountered no one.

A vague, prickly feeling on his chest and a sensation of pressure against his face alerted Spock that something solid lay ahead. He reached forward cautiously. His hands encountered a smooth metal surface, and his exploring fingertips told him it was a door. The surface was warm, warmer than the walls of the corridor. Spock hesitated, then leaned forward and placed his ear against the door. Faint noises, a groan cut short, then other noises which slowly receded into silence. All he could hear was a crackling sound that seemed naggingly familiar. Suddenly it struck him: fire.

Spock could afford to wait no longer in the interests of caution. The power failure that had freed him had also killed the sensors and motor that would have opened the door at his approach. He thrust his fingers into the narrow emergency slot, set his feet firmly, and heaved at the door with all his Vulcan strength. It slid open reluctantly on warped slots, the mechanism squealing in protest.

Now there was light—the flickering glow of a fire in the guardroom beyond the door. The blaze snapped and crackled at one corner of the otherwise dark room, a small fire but spreading rapidly, leaping to the wall hangings the Klingons affected even while Spock watched and rolling across the floor, feeding on the piles of smashed furniture. Spock headed quickly for the door at the far side of the room, holding his breath. The wreckage of what had been the room's electronic equipment crunched beneath his boots.

Spock was intent on getting out of the room in safety and then out of the building, but by the increasing glow of the fire, he noticed a Klingon lying on the floor, blood pooling beneath his head. The Vulcan stepped over to the prostrate guard quickly and knelt beside him. The Klingon was dead, or soon would be: from this close, Spock could see the multitude of bloody rips in the clothing, evidence of gashes and stab wounds beneath, and the misshapen head that surely meant a crushed skull. A fight of some sort? Spock asked himself. A mutiny of Klingon forces was unthinkable, but perhaps some sort of private grudge. But then, why hadn't the other Klingon simply used his phaser? Spock bent closer and examined the Klingon's head carefully. His analytical Vulcan mind was drawn by the mystery, and he knew he could hold his breath for some time yet, if necessary, so that the gases the fire must be producing were as yet no danger to him.

However, closer examination yielded nothing. The Klingon's head was covered with clotted blood, masking the true nature of the injury, and Spock finally decided that this was not the time or the place for an autopsy. Regretfully, he rose to his feet and left the room.

The hallway beyond was not utterly dark, for to one side lay another room with yet another fire burning in it. Spock quickly revised his estimate of his danger. He remembered enough of his trip through the building to the detention cell, he was sure, to be able to find his way out now. But the dark, punctuated only by the wavering, uncertain light from so many—surprisingly many—fires degraded even his orientation, and he found himself forced to exhale and draw another breath before he could find the exit. The gases he drew in affected him less than they would a human, but they did affect him, and Spock's quick analysis of his senses told him that he would not be able to carry on for much longer.

It was the shouting that led Spock to the exit. A multitude of voices, crying out in rhythmic unison; through the chant, despite the unintelligible alien sounds, ran an unmistakable exultation. He would have been drawn by the sound of voices in any case, as promising safety, but he was especially drawn by these, for they were the same fluid, whistling cries he had heard once before, on the beach with Kirk—the voices of Sealons.

Spock staggered through a smashed doorway into nighttime lit by the burning building behind him. He drew deep breaths gratefully, then turned to find that flames were now flaring out of every window and doorway of the huge office building. He turned away again, facing toward the darkness, and deliberately accelerated his eyes' dark adaptation. It took longer than it would otherwise have, because of the aftereffects of the glaring light of the fire at which he had just been looking, but after a moment a silent crowd of figures took shape out of the darkness. They were ranged in a rough line, parallel to the building's front, and just beyond the immediate glow of the fire. Their chanting had stopped, and they were gazing indecisively at the Vulcan.

Sealons, as Spock had anticipated. Not a Klingon was in sight: all dead within the building, Spock guessed, or else in hiding. Moments before, he had suddenly wondered whether the situation inside the building might be due to a Sealon uprising against their Klingon masters. Clearly that was the case. His main concern now was whether the Sealons would be able to distinguish him from the Klingons, or whether they would see no difference. He strode purposefully toward them.

As he drew close, they didn't move, apparently unintimidated. He stopped and stared at them, looking cocky and self-assured, but in fact not sure they would interpret his body language correctly. The Sealons had been almost standing—crouching, balancing on their haunches and the knuckles of their forepaws. Now, slowly, they all sank forward into their normal resting posture on land, lying almost prone, their powerful upper portions resting on their elbows. Spock knew this was as close to a backing down as he could hope for.

Spock stepped forward again, slowly this time but with determination. The Sealons shuffled aside to make room for him, the movement spreading across the ranks of dark, aquatic bodies like ripples. He walked forward steadily, the crowd of Sealons separating before him. Finally they stopped moving away; there was no sign of danger or defiance, but they simply refused to move out of his way. Before him rested a huge Sealon, still massive and powerful despite the sagging folds of skin around his mouth that probably signified advanced age. This one was still standing, or as close to it as a Sealon could manage on land, without the slightest sign of fear or hesitancy. Even without his great size and almost upright posture, which combined to make him tower above the others, there was an air of authority and self-confidence that made this Sealon stand out from the others. Despite his translator's inability to deal with the unknown Sealon language, Spock guessed that this was Matabele, the ruler of the Sealons who had made the mistake of inviting the Klingons in.

The Vulcan advanced slowly, raising his hand toward the Sealon's head. There was a stirring and growling among the other Sealons, but their ruler stayed where he was unflinching and allowed Spock to place his long fingers gently on his broad, frog-like face. The Vulcan mind-meld began.

Yes, it was Matabele. As the Sealon stiffened with amazement at the contact with the powerful Vulcan mind, Spock was sifting fascinatedly through the flood of images pouring into him from the brain of the Sealon. Clearly, this being and his culture were more complex than the Trellisanians had realized. But then a more specific image surfaced for a moment, and Spock grasped it quickly and fished urgently for the more submerged details. There! He had it. This uprising was part of something greater, and on Trellisane, even at this moment . . .

It was rare for the Klingons to overlook military details, but their long string of successes with subject peoples had made them overconfident, and it had come to seem impossible to them that anyone would even dream of revolting against their rule. The dome on the sea floor of Trellisane had no external defenses, since the Klingons knew the Trellisanians would not fight back and they simply did not think their tame Sealons would attack them.

When the environmental monitors indicated a leak in one segment of the dome, a call was automatically dispatched through the surrounding water for a Sealon maintenance team to repair any damage from the outside. The Sealon team leader quickly signaled back that he and his fellows were already at the site, working on the damaged area. Indeed, that was quite true, since it was that team of Sealons that had created the tear in the dome in the first place, and now they were clustered around the tear, working vigorously at enlarging it. Beneath them, on the other side of the tough fabric, were store rooms, and the Sealons were betting that the leak would therefore not be noticed directly by any Klingons, and that the monitoring computer would not send out a call for Klingon attention until it was too late. Occasionally one of them would have to swim up to the surface for air; then he would force himself quickly down again to rejoin his comrades sawing, cutting, even chewing away at the fabric of the dome. Elsewhere along the swelling, smooth surface, other groups of Sealons were doing the same. There were some waterproof bulkheads within the dome, and the Sealons wanted to be sure that there were no safe pockets of air left where Klingons might survive.

In his office within the dome, the Klingon officer who'd interviewed Kirk and Spock when they'd been taken prisoner was poring over some papers detailing the next steps he was to take. The conquest of the land would be gradual, by usual Klingon standards; that was largely to ensure that the Sealons weren't able to kill all Trellisanians off—the upper strata, the technically capable, were to be kept alive, for they could be of great service to Klingon in the future.

A sudden tremor shook the floor of his office and made the stylus lying near his hand roll back and forth. The Klingon frowned in surprise: Trellisane was supposed to be a geologically inactive world. He sneered at the thought. That probably had much to do with the Trellisanians' repellent timidity. Dismissing the matter as unimportant, he returned to the documents before him. Another, even sharper, tremor shook the room, and this time he rose from his chair and started toward the door, flaring into furious anger. It is Klingon nature to find an underling when something unpleasant happens and to blame and punish him for it, even if the unpleasant thing is utterly beyond his responsibility and control. The officer, disguising his deeply buried fear from himself as annoyance, stalked through the door to look for some lower ranking Klingon to punish.

He turned into the corridor and stopped. The air pressure shot up unbearably, lessened suddenly, and then shot up again. He fell to his knees clutching his ears in agony. Despite his ruined ears and his hands over them, he could hear a rush of sound in the abnormally dense air—a scream, and a roaring, thundering noise, then groaning, ripping sounds from the fabric of the building. The floor heaved violently, flinging him forward onto his face. Dazed, he got his hands underneath himself and raised himself, unwittingly imitating the common Sealon posture. The walls at the end of the corridor before him swelled inward and then burst, disappearing into the vast wave of foaming green seawater that rushed through. He opened his mouth to shout an order or a curse, but before any sound came out, the water smashed into him, carrying him before it like any other piece of flotsam, and crushed him against the farther walls of the corridor.

Only then did the water elsewhere in the dome reach the central power generators, and all lights went off, leaving the few Klingons who yet survived in trapped pockets of air in the dark. Their commander's body bobbed limply against the ceiling in his own office, up and down, as the sea's abrupt entry into one open room or corridor after another sent waves and ripples through the whole body of water inside the dome. Finally that ended and the water became still.

The Klingons who survived called out to each other cautiously and began to organize themselves, increasingly confident that, despite the pitch blackness, they could regroup and somehow escape. But their calls to each other provided all the signal the Sealons, inside the dome for the first time, needed. The silent, black water was their pathway to revenge. Not all the surviving Klingons were stabbed or bludgeoned to death. Some were dragged beneath the surface where crowds of Sealons, their eyes evolved to see dimly at these depths, could watch them struggle and drown.

* * *

Veedron put his hands over his face and groaned. "How awful! To die out there, under the sea."

McCoy snorted. "My heart bleeds for them." When Veedron had come to tell him of the huge bubbles filled with debris that had been seen bursting upon the surface of the sea and had said that Trellisianian experts were sure that it was a sign of the collapse of the Klingon's underwater base, McCoy had not tried to hide his pleasure. He still didn't try.

Veedron looked up at him in outrage and horror. "How can you be so callous? You're a medical man!"

McCoy nodded. "Yes, I'm a medical man. I'm also humane and compassionate, and I have a high empathy rating, which I try hard to hide beneath a crusty exterior. But I've also had many contacts with Klingons over the years, and I can tell you that the only good one is a dead one. To coin a cliché. If I hadn't felt that way before, what I've seen in this system would have convinced me."

Veedron was outraged. Before he could say anything, a messenger came into the room and muttered something to him. Veedron's face lost what little color it still had. "The Sealons are bringing the Klingon bodies ashore all along the coastline and leaving them just above the high tide line." He rose to his feet, his face suddenly brightening. "Perhaps this is their way of asking for help or offering peace!"

"They could contact you directly if they wanted to do that, Veedron. Don't be so naïve. I think this is a warning of what's in store for us, and also an attempt to intimidate us before the invasion begins. Undermine your courage, so to speak," McCoy added with heavy sarcasm. "I just wonder what they're waiting for." And I wonder why I've been waiting so long to initiate my own confrontation. "Veedron," McCoy said suddenly, not giving himself time for second thoughts, "I want to change the subject considerably. I've discovered that the *yegemot* have a brain implant of some kind put in them when they're children. Now, I know that you and your class have something like that, too, but I suspect they serve a very different function in your case."

"True," Veedron said distractedly. "Ours are for the purpose of communication."

"And theirs?"

"Oh." Veedron waved his hand. "For control."

"Hmm. There're different kinds of control, aren't there? Behavior control, population control . . . Those occur to me right away. What kind of control do you mean?"

Veedron shook off his distraction and stared at McCoy. "Why, for both of those, of course, as well as others. Come, come, Doctor: surely you've noticed how well discipline is maintained in our society."

So it's as bad as I feared, McCoy thought, remembering Veedron's vain attempt to discipline an impertinent Spenreed from whom the brain transplant had been removed, and remembering, too, a hole burned in a shelf. "So you give 'em the evil eye, and their brains get vaporized! Handy. The ancient Romans would've loved it." But what about that waiter who collapsed? Total brain death. He hadn't insulted anyone. And the capsules on the shelf—Spenreed talking about his death being forecast, or whatever. So it wasn't just a superstition. . . . "And you schedule lots of them for death even if they haven't' done anything to offend anyone, don't you?"

"Of course," Veedron said offhandedly. "I assumed you were aware of that."

"Aware of it! Scarcely! Hell, I thought you were civilized beings, not barbarians. You're worse than barbarians. They at least don't hide from the facts. When they kill each other, there's blood involved, and the killers know what they've done. You've tried to sanitize it, so that you can be coldblooded about being bloodthirsty, and all the while you can pretend that you're not doing anything out of the ordinary. They just drop to the floor, nice and clean, and you go on about your business. And then I suppose the bodies have to be carried away by other *yegemots,* poor bastards. And all this time, you've been trying to pretend to us that you're somehow better than the Sealons."

Veedron responded with anger of his own. "Who are you to assume a pose of moral superiority? We made you and your shipmates welcome on our world, and you partook gladly enough of our hospitality. You ate our meat with us, and yet you must have known how ritually and symbolically important that is to us."

McCoy was thrown off balance by this seeming *non sequitur.* "We knew that you're vegetarians, mostly. I don't understand."

Veedron sneered. "Then it's time you did. Come with me." He grasped McCoy's arm and pulled him from the room. Ignoring McCoy's protests and struggles, and displaying a surprising strength, he dragged the Earthman along behind him. They hurried down corridors until they were outside the building.

Still moving, Veedron pulled McCoy down a quiet street, a beautiful avenue marred by the rubble of an earlier Sealon attack. To McCoy's repeated and increasingly angry questions, Veedron at last replied that they were going to observe food preparation, and then he would say no more. Finally they reached a small, isolated building that seemed to be Veedron's destination. Breathing heavily, the Trellisanian paused for a moment before it, and then he strode into the building, still dragging McCoy behind him. A sickeningly familiar smell attacked McCoy; he knew what it must be, but he refused to admit that truth to himself.

They entered a large, high-ceilinged room. A group of Trellisanians stood with their backs to the door, hard at work, hands rising and falling steadily. By the noise and the motion, they were chopping. They became aware of the presence of the newcomers, and some of them turned to see who it was. They knew Veedron, of course, and one of them came forward to greet him subserviently. Now McCoy could see everything.

The men wore butcher's aprons, and they were spattered with blood. Beyond them was a long table, and upon it lay a dismembered corpse. And in a far corner of the room, McCoy now became aware, halves and quarters of torsos hung upon a row of hooks.

Chapter Eighteen

"Too late!" Karox growled, slapping his palm against the yielding arm of his command chair. "Too late. The Romulans know we're approaching their territory."

The peremptory challenge had come over the ship's communications a moment earlier. Karox and his ship had stayed well beyond the sensor range of the Romulan ships they were pursuing, but the Romulans were now beyond the boundaries of the Neutral Zone, and the Romulans had powerful installations along that frontier to watch for approaching vessels. These installations had detected the Klingon approach and issued the challenge. That Karox had not foreseen this was strong evidence to Kirk that the Klingon captain's confidence and relaxation were masks for a worry and tension that were interfering with his judgment.

"I'm not ready to fight them," Karox muttered. "I'll have to stop soon to avoid penetrating the Zone, and if I do that, the *Enterprise* will escape from me. I'll have to attack now, risk a war."

"Wait!" Kirk said. "Release me. Take me to your transporter room. You can send me to the *Enterprise* before she's out of range. Her shields are down, and the Romulans won't be expecting that. I'll bring her back out."

Karox looked at him with scorn and anger, but then his expression changed suddenly. "Yes. With Klingon guards to go with you." He sat up, his chest swelling, eyes blazing. "I won't destroy the *Enterprise*—I'll *capture* her! My most glorious victory." He barked a string of commands.

Kirk's wrists were freed, and then he was pulled to his feet and marched quickly from the bridge and through a short but bewildering series of intersecting corridors. At the end, he found himself in what was obviously a transporter room, much like the one on the *Enterprise*, but larger, as most things were on this ship, with many more transmission stations.

There was a short delay, and then three heavily armed and heavily muscled Klingons marched in and took up positions wordlessly on the stations beside Kirk's. Karox entered the room.

"Kirk. I know this handful of men isn't enough to take over the *Enterprise*, but they *are* enough to keep an eye on you and control the bridge. When you're back in command, bring her out and surrender her to me. If you betray me, they'll kill you and I'll destroy your ship. Well?"

Kirk nodded. He understood the conditions well enough and accepted them only because he had no choice.

Karox motioned to the technician at the transporter console. The man's fingers moved rapidly over the keyboard, and Karox's sneering face faded from Kirk's view.

The elevator door opened and the four-being group creature came onto the bridge unnoticed by those already there. The Chapel component moved quietly in one direction, and the other three rolled off the other way.

It was Sulu who noticed them first, catching a movement from the corner of his eye. He looked up quickly to see the three Onctiliians bearing down on one of the Assassins, the one still standing close to Hander Morl. The thought flashed through Sulu's mind in an instant that this weird creature, who had been brought up from the surface of Trefolg, must be in some way on the side of the *Enterprise* crew now; even if not, its attack on its former comrade could only help Sulu and his friends. Even though Sulu managed to stifle the exclamation which had risen to his lips at first, Hander Morl had noticed his astonished expression and had followed the direction of Sulu's gaze.

Morl turned his chair around just in time to see the Assassin crumple before the Onctiliians' unexpected assault. Then the Onctiliians changed direction and charged toward Morl. But Morl was already in motion, flinging himself desperately from his chair.

The new mental integration with Chapel was complete, but physically the three were still not quite balanced, missing the contribution of their dead partner and slightly disoriented by the need to reconcile visual images from two physically separate locations, theirs and Chapel's. They crashed into the chair, bending its base so that it spun about at a crazy angle. But they could no longer redirect themselves quickly enough or move fast enough to catch Morl, who scrambled frantically along the floor, then pulled himself across Sulu's console.

The bridge had erupted into life, with personnel shouting at each other and trying to keep out of the way of the Onctiliians. The Chapel component stepped up to the side of one of the Nactern warriors, moving warily because the memories provided by the Onctiliian components revealed how deadly a threat the Nactern could be to the safety of the Earthwoman body. She pressed a hypodermic against the Nactern's side, pressing the trigger as she did so. The Nactern whirled about, hands coming up for a fatal chop; but her legs wilted beneath her even as she turned, and she collapsed heavily to the deck. The other Nactern sprang to her side, oblivious to Chapel's presence or the maneuverings of Morl and the Onctiliians.

The Assassin standing near Scott stepped forward to enter the fight, and Scott, breathing a quick and silent prayer, stuck out a foot so that the man tripped over it and fell forward into the depression holding the command chair. Scott was on him before he could get up again, chopping repeatedly at the back of his neck. The Assassin slumped forward with a groan, unconscious, and Scott rose to his feet, breathing heavily, but inordinately pleased with himself. "Don't mess with *my* engines, laddie," he muttered.

Hander Morl and the Onctiliians were moving about the console cluster in a deadly dance that struck Chekov as curiously stately. Morl's phaser had fallen out during his mad dash to get out of the Onctiliians' path, and he had not been able to get back to it. It lay unnoticed on the floor near the command chair, and Morl could not see how he could reach it. Meanwhile, he circled the consoles slowly, trying to keep them between him and the Onctiliians. He wanted to call for help, but some instinct told him, even though he was afraid to take his eyes from the Onctiliians to look around the bridge, that he was on his own. He grasped the console nearest him for support, his knees shaking with the fear that overwhelmed him.

Step by step, placing one foot carefully after the other, Morl forced himself into motion again. He passed behind Chekov's seat, but his eyes were fixed on the menacing ball of flesh; it had no visible eyes, but Morl could *feel* its gaze following his every movement. Chekov jumped from his chair and shoved Morl away from the consoles. Morl stumbled and fell heavily onto the floor, well away from the shelter of the consoles. He saw the Onctiliians rolling toward him; he slithered toward his phaser, lying nearby, but knew he wouldn't be able to reach it in time.

A phaser beam sliced across the bridge and trans-fixed the Onctiliians. The Nactern warrior, satisfied that her comrade and lover was only unconscious and not harmed, had at last turned her attention to the excitement around her. Seeing Morl cringing back as the Onctiliians rushed toward him, she had drawn her phaser quickly and fired at her former ally. The Onctiliians glowed white and disappeared: the final, ultimate disruption of union and communion. Chapel screamed at the same instant and sank down nervelessly.

Morl rose shakily to his feet, his face drained of all color, clutching his phaser. He pointed it at Chekov. "You tried to kill me!" he screamed. The gun was waving so wildly that he could not keep it aimed at the young Russian, and he had to grip it with both hands in order to point it properly. "You," he screamed again, but his throat constricted with fear and fury and he couldn't get any more words out.

The Nactern warrior stepped forward in front of Chekov, shielding him. She held her arms out to either side. "No, Hander," she said simply.

Morl, his hands still shaking, fired. The beam caught the Nactern full in the chest. For an instant, just before she vanished in the glow of disruption, Morl saw a look of surprise and accusation cross her face.

Morl sat down heavily in the command chair. Because of its tilted base, the chair swiveled under him and dumped him on the floor. The horror and self-hatred on Morl's face made what might otherwise have been a bizarrely comic incident into tragedy. Sulu, Chekov, and the others on the bridge watched Morl's collapse into tears with something approaching pity. His follower, his subordinate, entrusted to him and trusting in him! She had not been a sacrifice to the cause, like the Onctiliian: she had been killed by a stupid accident, by his doing, through his own inepti-tude and stupidity. That was the kind of leader he really was: inept to the point that he endangered his own people, or even killed them himself through sheer clumsiness. Kirk would not have done something like that, he admitted to himself; Kirk and these other Star Fleet personnel he'd been dealing with would never be guilty of this kind of failure. He knew that the pain of remorse was not enough to give him the punishment he felt he deserved.

Four shapes twinkled into existence on the bridge. The *Enterprise* personnel, still rocked by all that had happened to them, were scarcely able to react to this latest shock. The twinkling lights resolved themselves into James Kirk and his Klingon guards. The Klingons had their guns already drawn, and they arranged themselves quickly along one side of the bridge, guns covering the Federation personnel.

Kirk glanced around quickly, trying to size up the situation. "Mr. Scott?"

"Sir. *Enterprise* secure internally but within Romulan space. Do you have orders?"

Kirk turned to the Klingons behind him. "As you can see, gentlemen, the *Enterprise* is already under Federation control again. Thus by boarding you are risking war with the Federation as well as with the Romulans. I'd advise you to put away your weapons and accept the situation gracefully." He could almost feel the growing tension behind him, the instinctive reaction of the crew to the presence of Klingons, armed, aboard their ship. If the Klingons didn't back down, and soon, someone would make a move, breaking the tense restraint, and then the situation would be beyond his control.

The Klingon squad leader hesitated, his instinctive hatred of humans warring with his prudence and sense of duty. He had the humans at a disadvantage, confident that three Klingons with weapons drawn were immeasurably superior to any number of soft and unarmed humans. And yet he was an ambitious young officer, and he suspected that Kirk was right about the legal situation. If he acted hostilely anyway and Kirk *was* right, then he would suffer both loss of rank and further, and probably painful, punishment. He decided the risk was probably too great. Another thought struck him suddenly. Success on Kirk's side could scarcely help Karox's career, and with Karox out of the way, the squad leader stood a good chance of moving up a step or two in rank. He holstered his phaser and motioned his men to do the same.

Kirk released a breath he hadn't realized he'd been holding. "Lieutenant Uhura, contact the commander of the Romulan fleet that has us under tractor beam." While Uhura moved to comply, Kirk said to the Klingon squad leader, "And I want you to contact Karox and explain to him what the situation is here."

The Klingon uttered an exclamation of surprise.

Kirk grinned at him. "That's right. Tell him. And also tell him that he'll have to beam over here himself immediately to settle this situation once and for all."

The Klingon officer looked openly doubtful, but he drew his small communicator from his belt nonetheless and spoke into it quietly. The voice that replied was far from quiet: Kirk could hear Karox's miniaturized bellows from across the bridge. But the Klingon captain had little choice, Kirk knew, except to give up entirely on ever getting the *Enterprise* under his control. Sooner than giving up so readily what Karox had hoped would be his greatest victory, Kirk hoped, he would risk coming aboard the *Enterprise* in person, even though she was now under Federation control onboard and under Romulan control from the outside.

The Romulans had at first refused to respond to Uhura, fearing that another betrayal like the first one was on tap. Eventually, however, she received a grudging reply, and then Kirk took over. "This is James T. Kirk, commanding the *U.S.S. Enterprise*," he rapped out, glorying in the words, in being able to say them again. "I must speak to your fleet commander immediately."

After a pause, a new voice boomed out over the bridge, calm, unperturbed, strong—Romulan. "This is Tal, fleet commander. You have much to answer for, James T. Kirk. You tricked us twice before, but you will not do so again. You misled the brave woman who was my commander, leading her to weakness, dishonor, and death. And you murdered my warriors most cowardly and unfairly. You must be taken where you and your crew can be punished properly."

Tal: Kirk had dealt with him before, during the incident Tal had referred to, but then Tal had been only a subcommander. He must have distinguished himself to have risen, in the relatively short time that had passed, to command of a fleet of ships entrusted with this sensitive mission. Despite all the differences between the Federation and the Romulan Empire, Kirk knew that such a rise must require the sort of professional competence and dedication a similar advancement would require in Star Fleet. This was a man much like him, one he could respect and admire; an equal. It occurred to him, not for the first time, that there was a kind of professional community building between the stars; he and his crew had more in common with the commanders and crews of the Romulan ships, and even with Karox and the Klingons under him, than they did with the teeming millions confined to the surfaces of the many planets that made up the Federation. Kirk smiled slightly. "Fleet Commander Tal, congratulations on your promotion. Considering your high rank, I'm sure you have been told something about the activity in the Trellisane-Sealon system. You'll agree that that situation is more important to your empire's well-being than taking revenge on me and my crew."

"We have monitored your communications recently," Tal said reluctantly. "And those of the Klingons in this area. We know you are both heavily involved in some sort of local war there. However, that scarcely affects us. You are no threat to us at this moment, and the Klingons have assured us they have no ambitions in our space."

Kirk laughed. "And you believed them, of course?"

There was a long pause before Tal answered. "What do you want to discuss with me?" he said cautiously.

Kirk relaxed, aware only now that he had been holding himself tensely until this moment. "Not only with you, Tal, but with the Klingon commander of a ship you can't even see as well."

"Can't even see? What are you talking about, Kirk?"

"They can detect your ships from beyond your sensor range. Chew that over for a while. While you're digesting that fact, arrange to have yourself beamed over here for a three-way, face-to-face conference. We have something important to arrange, and I think it can be done more quickly and satisfactorily by three commanders like us than by distant governments."

"I will be there," Tal said simply.

After you dispatch a message to your home base to tell them what's happened and about the Klingons' new superiority, you mean, Kirk added mentally. That was something that Romulans seemed to lack, compared to both humans and Klingons: the willingness to break out of their rigid adherence to duty and obedience and display some independence, some autonomy. It was their strength as an empire, but their weakness as individuals. If the war between the Romulans and the Federation ever started up again, that might provide Kirk and his fellow officers with the edge they needed.

Kirk turned to find himself face to face with a grinning chief engineer. "Captain," Scott said, his burr returning for a moment, "we've been busy. Look." He pointed at the command chair, which a crew of two technicians from Engineering were just finishing with, having replaced its base with a spare and reconnected the communications leads.

Kirk grinned back at him and sat down gratefully in his command chair. "Fits perfectly, Mr. Scott. Thank you."

Scott looked faintly sheepish. "Och. Welcome back, sir."

A growl from the direction of the squad of Klingons drew Kirk's attention. Karox had arrived and was standing in the midst of his men, being briefed on recent events by the squad leader. He pushed the squad leader away angrily and stalked over to face Kirk. "Kirk!" he snarled. "Why did you tell them about our new long-range sensors? What treason are you up to?"

Kirk smiled at him, knowing it would only increase the Klingon's fury. "You're stretching the meaning of that word quite a bit, Karox. It's not treason for me to neutralize your advantage a bit. Relax and enjoy our hospitality. The Romulan commander will be beaming over here shortly, and then the three of us will have a few things to discuss."

Karox howled his anger. "Kirk, it won't work! I know what you're up to, but Trellisane and Sealon are ours now, and you're not going to deprive us of the system."

"I think events have overtaken you, Karox. Surpassed you, perhaps. There are situations that Klingon bluster and aggression cannot master. You will have to realize that you face such a situation here. You know Klingon forces cannot face an alliance of Federation and Romulan ships, and that's just what you'll have to contend with if you don't cooperate."

Karox drew back, his face relaxing. "Yes," he nodded, speaking calmly. "Neither of you has the courage to face us alone. I believe you would combine to defeat us, because you each fear us so."

Kirk shrugged. "Put it in those terms, if it preserves your self-respect. The results are what matter to me. Consider this, too, Karox." Kirk sat forward in his chair. "You could be the one who pulls a stalemate, at worst, out of what is otherwise shaping up as a disaster for Klingon. You won't retain the Trellisane-Sealon system for long if you alarm the Romulans as much as you've already alarmed the Federation. I'm offering you the chance—you, personally—to retain some promising options for Klingon, instead of losing the system unequivocally."

Karox grew thoughtful. "Yes," he nodded, a smile growing on his dark face. "Yes, Kirk, you're right. I would be a hero, and . . . certain others . . . would be villains. Yes," he laughed loudly, "yes, it grows more appealing by the second."

Kirk disguised his scorn. "Good, Karox. I think we have our third negotiator now." The preliminary signs of a transporter beam transference had appeared on the bridge not far from him and Karox. The lean form of Tal, so startlingly like Spock's, began to take shape. The pointed ears, the sharp features, remnants of the Romulans' Vulcan ancestry—Kirk knew he'd have to guard himself carefully during the upcoming negotiations, lest those Romulan features mislead him unconsciously into being overly trusting. This was no Vulcan; this was a Romulan, a deadly enemy, as deadly in his way as Karox and the other Klingons. Kirk rose to his feet and uttered some formal words of welcome, meanwhile thinking that what was to come might be harder than any physical battle he had ever fought. "Tal, Karox, please follow me. Mr. Sulu, you have the con. I will be in the conference room with our two guests, and I do *not* want to be disturbed."

Chapter Nineteen

Sealons are not given to psychological warfare. Direct, physical, frontal attack has always been their favorite method of making war, the attacks launched as soon as the warring parties feel adequately prepared—or even before, if the blood lust and desire for conquest are stronger than their rudimentary feelings of caution. Even Pongol and Matabele, the greatest leaders and organizers in Sealon history, greater rulers than any of the heroes in Sealon's many sagas, were never able to change this basic nature. Pongol and Matabele led their nation to triumph over its neighbors, not by using the gentle arts of persuasion on their subjects, but rather by having greater strength of will, more dominating personalities, than those among their advisers and subchiefs who opposed their plans. They simply imposed their own ideas of strategy upon their followers, brooking no opposition. Thus the long quiescence of the Sealons in the seas of Trellisane was highly uncharacteristic.

It was also completely destructive of what little morale remained among the Trellisanians. Had the Sealons been intending to conduct psychological warfare, and had they known enough about the working of Trellisanians' minds to do so, they could not have done better than to wait beneath the calm sea surface as they did. Even the *yegemot*, whose defiance had already diminished as their numbers dwindled at Sealon hands, became quiet, waiting uncertainly for the next move from the deadly invader hidden beneath the seas.

Veedron's reservoir of courtliness had deserted him. "How *can* we get more organized?" he screamed at McCoy. "We don't know what to organize *for!*"

McCoy shrugged and pressed his palms against his eyes. He felt enormous fatigue, and he seemed to be incapable of feeling anything else. It was as if the long, hard, thankless hours of dealing with Trellisane's increasingly uncooperative leaders and the nausea resulting from his latest discovery had drained him of even the ability to experience anything but weariness. He let his hands fall to the table. "I don't know what to tell you, Veedron. Perhaps it's not worth doing anything, after all. We're all doomed. Give up and face the inevitable. I know *I* don't care any more."

This was enough to at last reduce Veedron to silence. He stared at McCoy, realizing for perhaps the first time just how much of himself this alien had given to Trellisane, how unselfishly he had given it—and how little thanks he had received for his sacrifice. Veedron searched for the words to apologize to McCoy and to thank him: if they must all perish, then Veedron wished all the more to restore Trellisane's honor before it was too late. Before he could formulate the long, elaborate circumlocution he intended to deliver, however, a *yegemot* entered the room and hurried over to him.

"A ship, Your Honor," the man said breathlessly. "A ship of the Sealons has arrived."

Veedron glared at him. "You interrupted me for that, creature?" he snapped. "More invasion forces, that's all."

"Sir, this one has come down on the ground near here, not in the sea."

Veedron exchanged a glance of surprise with McCoy.

"Either they're overwhelmed with confidence," McCoy said, "or they want to talk to us."

Veedron shook his head. "They could have done that earlier. A special ship from Sealon wasn't necessary."

"Then maybe there's someone special onboard, someone the Sealons here have been waiting for."

"Matabele," Veedron muttered. He turned to the *yegemot* messenger. "Take me to the landing site," he ordered. He turned back to McCoy, his tone of voice respectful. "Do you wish to come with me, Doctor?"

"I wouldn't miss this for the world!" He had noticed Veedron's changed manner. It was almost back to the politeness of earlier days, before Veedron's revelation concerning the slaves. Wonder how he'd act if he knew I've been taking those damned capsules out of every slave I can get my hands on. . . .

The landing site was near the Sealon-blasted subspace transceiver Veedron had shown Kirk and Spock some days earlier. McCoy had never seen this place before, and now his attention was drawn to the huge vessel resting in the midst of what had once been parkland, rather than to what was left of the recreation ground. There was no activity around the great vessel; a crowd of Trellisanians watched nervously from a distance, waiting for someone in a position of sufficient authority, such as Veedron, to show up and take over.

As he and McCoy approached, one of the watching Trellisanians broke away and hurried up to them. It was one of the doctors working under McCoy, and he addressed himself to the Federation doctor rather than to Veedron. If Veedron had been an Earthman, he might have resented this, but as a Trellisanian, and especially as the chief of the Protocol Binders, he gave way to McCoy's position of authority almost instinctively.

"There is no sign of life at all, Doctor. I happened to see the ship coming down, and I came here immediately in case I was needed, but no one has been injured. This crowd gathered fairly quickly; however, the Sealons have not attacked it. The ship could be automatically operated, for all I've seen."

McCoy thanked the man absentmindedly and walked toward the Sealon ship, scarcely noticing the crowd of Trellisanians parting respectfully for him.

He had never seen a spacegoing vessel this large down on the surface of a planet before. The largest vessels he had seen on the ground in previous experience were shuttles, such as those of the *Enterprise*. This enormous mass of metal, resting quietly on the ground, had the indefinable aura of deep space about it, that place where he had already spent so much of his life. The ship sat lightly, as if it were ready at any moment, at any hint of a command from its masters, to leap joyously back into space, its proper home. McCoy had spent the days on Trellisane immersed in the details of his grim duty—body counts and hospital beds, limited manpower and nonexistent medicines—and until this moment had not thought about space. It was his proper home, too, he realized, and the ship was a magnet to him. Did the Sealons love space, too? Was that why their ship spoke so eloquently of the beauty of the great blackness? Why, then, he had some things in common with them, after all, perhaps more than he had with that crowd of jellyfish muttering nervously behind him. He walked forward slowly. Veedron called out to him: "Doctor, please be careful!" And then louder: "Doctor!" But McCoy ignored him and kept walking toward the Sealon ship. Matabele: there must be a man—no, a being—he could admire and respect, certainly more so than he could feel anything of such emotions toward Veedron or the other *gemot* leaders.

At the base of the ship, a door slid open, eliciting a gasp from the Trellisanians. McCoy stopped moving, overcome himself, at last, with the realization that he had not behaved with prudence in exposing himself this way. He was well away from the crowd, alone in the space directly before the Sealon ship, and he would be the obvious first target if Sealon warriors should emerge from that silent facade and launch an attack.

A ramp slowly extended itself from the bottom of the doorway, covering the short drop to the ground. A man could have jumped down with no trouble, as could a Klingon. This, McCoy realized, was an adaptation so that Sealons, whose bodies he had already examined carefully, could slide to the ground without injuring their small, weak legs. At last he would meet some live Sealons, perhaps Matabele himself. So what if he was about to die? He would at least go bravely, even adventurously, perhaps in combat with the great Sealon king himself.

The sunlight was bright, while the space beyond the doorway was quite dim. A figure appeared in the opening, but McCoy could not make it out. Then it stepped forward onto the ramp and descended calmly to the ground to stand before McCoy, and the doctor opened his mouth in astonishment but found himself unable to speak.

"I trust you are well, Doctor, and that your speechlessness has no pathological cause?" Mr. Spock asked.

The negotiations were taking place in a large room onboard the Sealon ship, and they were not going well.

A raised platform had been constructed near the door for the Trellisanians' use and provided with comfortable chairs and a small table. The sunken floor of the room was covered with a meter and a half of water, and it was here that the Sealons relaxed during the discussions. Their great shapes, far more fluid and graceful in the water than on a dry surface, flowed swiftly back and forth across the room. Against a far wall, Matabele rested on the surface of the water, huge and silent, raising himself occasionally to stare at the Trellisanians with his penetrating, discerning, discomforting gaze. Sealons normally squint in sunlight, but here in the gloomy, humid interior of the ship, Matabele's eyes were wide open, huge, black, and impenetrable. The Sealon negotiators would carry the words of the Trellisanians to him, receive his instructions, and then dart back across the room to the platform to resume the bargaining.

Spock, drawing on knowledge gained during the intimacy of the mind-meld, had managed to reprogram both his and McCoy's translators to handle the fluid, whistling speech of the Sealons. Thus communication was possible through the medium of the two Star Fleet officers even though none of the few Trellisanians who knew the Sealon speech was available. Matabele had already sent messages to his forces in the seas to halt their interference with Trellisanian communications; thus Veedron and the other *gemot* leaders were once again in contact with those of their equals who survived on the other continents. However, it had proven far easier for Spock to work out such practical details of communication than it was to design a settlement acceptable to both Trellisanians and Sealons.

The Trellisanians in fact had nothing to bargain with, and they knew it, and this had elicited in the *gemot* leaders a sudden and surprising stubbornness founded on wounded pride. Matabele demanded that the seas of Trellisane, most of its small island chains, and certain inlets along the continental coasts be given to his people. In fact, all of this and far more was already his for the taking, if he chose that route. In return, Matabele offered extensive fishing rights in what would become, under the agreement, sovereign Sealon territory on Trellisane and even in the oceans of Sealon. The oceans of the two worlds were the only territories attractive to the Sealons; as far as Matabele was concerned, large land surfaces, including the moons of the system and whatever other planetary surfaces Trellisanian technology could make habitable, were free for

Trellisane to take. Above all, the increasingly techno-logical Sealons would become trading partners and peaceful allies of Trellisane.

The agreement proposed by Matabele was so balanced and logical that McCoy was sure he saw a Vulcan mind behind it. He leaned toward Spock and whispered to him, "You've been a busy little boy, haven't you, Spock? Just what have you been up to since I saw you last?"

Spock cast a short glance of annoyance at him and turned his attention back to the Trellisanian *gemot* leaders. It was clear to him that it was the very magnanimity of Matabele's offer that offended them. If they had shown this sort of backbone earlier, he reflected, they might not be in this situation now; as it was, their argumentativeness was little more than petulance. "I think, sir," Spock said calmly to Veedron, "that the Sealon terms are more than generous."

Veedron glared at him. "How do we know we can even trust these animals to keep their word? Agreements don't mean the same to them as they do to you or me."

Part of the Trellisanian anger, Spock realized, was a way of masking a particular and peculiar fear: to survive under the proposed agreement, Trellisane would have to move outward into its system aggressively, expand rapidly and with determination, colonizing moons and planets wherever possible. Veedron and his colleagues feared this prospect more, perhaps, than they feared annihilation. Indeed, perhaps their fear-filled, retiring souls would welcome destruction as the ultimate escape from challenge and responsibility. "Sir," Spock said firmly, in a tone that made it clear that even Vulcan patience has its limits, "you do not speak for all the people of Trellisane, but only for those who are members of *gemots*. There are fishermen and other slaves, as I know quite well, who belong to no *gemot* and who would welcome total control of this world, even under Sealon terms."

"Yes, indeed," McCoy chimed in, scarcely able to keep a grin off his face. "And for that matter, why aren't they represented here?"

"You're quite right, Doctor," Spock said gravely. "A serious oversight on my part. I should have arranged for the presence of a member of the slave class."

The Trellisanians all began talking at the same time. McCoy was finally able to impose silence on them and gain their attention by pounding his fist on the light table, which jumped off the floor in response, and shrieking, "Shut up!" at them at the top of his voice. They obeyed him largely because they were stunned that someone they had recently grown to respect as an equal could be guilty of such a breach of etiquette. Spock stared at McCoy with a hint of amusement on his almost expressionless features. The high-pitched communications at the far end of the room ceased and Matabele and his subordinates turned their dark eyes and froglike faces toward McCoy.

"Well," McCoy said, affecting heartiness, "now that you're listening, I think I'd better point out a few things to you." He drew a deep breath. "There are two facts you of the *gemots* need to consider. First of all, you need our protection—the Federation's, I mean— whether or not you decide to become members, and you must have realized from what I've already told you that you won't be able to get it with your present governmental setup. You'll have to rearrange things so that the *yegemot* have a voice.

"Second, as Mr. Spock has already pointed out, the *yegemot* themselves won't accept the *status quo*. They've fought the Sealons. They've tried to defend this world, and you can bet they didn't risk their lives—lose them, in too many cases—just to save your privileges. You know, I've been a busy little boy.

Removing brain implants, for instance . . . Face it, gentlemen: you have no choice."

Veedron licked his lips and looked around at his fellow *gemot* leaders, but they all looked down at the table, refusing to meet his eyes. At last, convinced his colleagues would not offer him any support, Veedron spoke. "Doctor, I know those arguments," he said reluctantly. "I've used them with myself. I suppose I—we—would be willing to accept a small degree of participation in the government by the *yegemot*, since we seem to have little choice, were it not for one insurmountable difficulty." He stopped, his evident distaste for the subject seemingly making it almost impossible for him to say more.

"And that difficulty is?" Spock prompted.

Veedron forced himself to continue. "They are animals, beasts." Anger flared in him again at the thought. "They serve us because they were bred up from bestiality for that purpose only! We can't—"

"Just a moment," McCoy cut in, his face stern. "You tried that one on me before, and this time I can't just let it go by. As soon as you confirmed that you and the *yegemot* are cross-fertile, I knew the story about their ancestry was rubbish. If your medical men weren't as prejudiced as the rest of you, they'd have drawn the same conclusions as I did. It could be proved easily enough with tissue samples in a lab, but that's not even necessary: you have to have common ancestors, and fairly recently, you have to still be the same species—by definition—to be able to breed together."

The Trellisanians were speechless. McCoy wondered whether the cause were confusion or outrage. He became aware for the first time of Matabele and his Sealons watching the scene with a calculating silence. One of the Trellisanians finally found his voice. "But your colleague, the Vulcan . . . I was told he's half Earthman. What you said is obviously not true." The rest of the group nodded vigorously and muttered their agreement.

"Sorry to destroy your last defense," McCoy said, feeling like a hypocrite because he wasn't sorry at all, "but Vulcans and Earthmen are both descended from an ancient race who colonized most of the known Galaxy. Almost all the humanoid races we know of are descended from them, and that probably includes you. Of course there has been genetic drift and adaptation to extreme conditions, producing anomalies like the Vulcans. The races who don't have those common ancestors are precisely those races who are not cross-fertile with humanoids from other worlds."

Veedron said, "This is a great deal to ask us to accept, Doctor. To overturn the ways of generations on your word . . ." He shook his head.

"Damn it," McCoy flared at him, "I'm not asking you to take just my word! When you first told me that cockeyed theory about the *yegemot* being bred up from domestic animals, I went right out and collected tissue samples from various corpses, victims of the bombardments, both *yegemot* and your own kind. The results are all available for your biologists, well documented, genetic analyses and everything. You could have done that yourselves at any time. Now I've done it for you. Now you'll have to face the truth!" McCoy realized he was on his feet and shouting. Feeling suddenly foolish, he fell silent and sat down.

Spock's almost-smile was even more apparent to McCoy. "Well?" he snapped at the Vulcan. "Do you have something to add on the subject?"

"Not at this moment, Doctor." Spock added in a low voice, "Implants? You must explain that to me later." He turned to the Trellisanians. "I don't think you'd be wise to put off your decision much longer, gentlemen. I've come to know Matabele quite intimately," he paused, darting images of chasing small prey in the dark, deep oceans of Sealon surfacing in his memory, ". . . intimately, and I believe that despite his pragmatism and *magnanimity*," he emphasized the word, "the usual Sealon impatience is very much a part of him. If you delay any longer, he might withdraw his offer and launch the final attack. His followers in the seas must be chafing at the delay as it is."

Perhaps it was the thought of murderous Sealons swarming out of the seas, slithering across the beaches to kill and destroy, perhaps it was the cumulative effect of Spock's well orchestrated attack; whatever the cause, defeat was evident on the faces of the Trellisanians. Even though they performed the ritual of discussing their reply among themselves and with the invisible host of other *gemot* leaders linked to them mind-to-mind, the result was clear long before they announced it. At last, with a deep sigh, Veedron said to Spock, "Please tell the king we accept his terms."

Before Spock could say anything to the expectant Sealons, who were now swimming back and forth impatiently near the platform, McCoy raised his hand to stop him. "And what about *our* terms concerning the *yegemot?*"

An expression of great distaste crossed Veedron's face. "Yes, we agree to your terms as well."

Spock turned toward the Sealons and spoke a few words quietly in Vulcan. His voice was drowned out by the fluting, whistling sounds that came from his translator and sent the Sealons gliding swiftly across the room to tell Matabele that the oceans of Trellisane were his.

The Sealons erupted into wild gyrations of triumph, flashing across the room and leaping out of the water in front of the platform, whistling shrilly, and splashing the Trellisanians as they crashed back into the water.

A new Sealon arrival darted in through the doorway, looked around for a moment until he spotted his king, and then glided swiftly to Matabele. At first the Trellisanians and the two Federation officers on the platform didn't notice the new Sealon, partly because all Sealons looked alike to them, and partly because the Trellisanians were too busy wiping water off themselves and rearranging their robes. Those on the platform finally realized that something important had happened when the Sealons, Matabele in the lead, churned through the doorway and vanished, leaving behind a trail of bubbles and foam that slowly dissipated.

"I think, Veedron, that we'd better return to your headquarters," Spock said. He rose and led the way to the exit, using the narrow ledges that ran along the walls just above water level. The Trellisanians followed spiritlessly, defeat heavy upon them, as if nothing they did mattered any more.

Outside, it was already dark and the crowd had drifted away. The group made its way as quickly as possible to the headquarters building of the Protocol Binders *gemot*. The building gleamed in the dark, every light on, and people hurried in and out. The illusion of organized pandemonium was shattered when they entered: there was no organization, only pandemonium.

Spock tried unsuccessfully to stop passersby to find out what had happened. Veedron finally succeeded when one of the hurrying functionaries recognized him. "Sir," the man said breathlessly, "I'm glad you're back. We've all been worried—"

"Never mind that. What's caused this excitement?"

"You don't know?" He looked at the impatient faces before him and explained quickly. "A fleet of ships just arrived. Klingons, Romulans, the Federation— combined. They're in orbit now, demanding that we and the Sealons surrender to them!"

Chapter Twenty

Captain's Log: Stardate 7532.8

> The *Enterprise* will be leaving Trellisane orbit for
> Starbase 28 in a matter of moments. Upon arriv-
> al, I will deliver our surviving prisoners. I will also
> dump to the Starbase diplomatic computer the
> full details of the accord I have signed with the
> Romulans and Klingons.

Kirk raised his thumb from the log recorder button
and let his mind drift for a moment. Would Star Fleet
Command and the Federation Council accept the new
treaty with only minor quibbling? Or would his actions
be condemned as an overreaching of his authority? He
shrugged and pressed the log recorder on again.

"Perhaps this is the beginning of the cooperation
between us and the Klingons forecast by the Organians.
It goes beyond that forecast by including the Romulans
as well." Kirk hesitated, then, grinning, added, "This is
surely one of the most significant opportunities for
peace we have had in this century, and I sincerely hope
we will not fail to grasp it." He released the button to
off and sat back, feeling satisfied. "Helm, initiate new
course on this orbit."

"Aye, Captain."

Back in control, Kirk thought with satisfaction. Giving orders again, the orders that moved this enormous machine and its 400-odd crewmen—a different kind of machine—sending it across the Galaxy if he, James T. Kirk, simply desired it. The surge of power from the engines, the faint vibration under his feet: it was all in obedience to his will; the ship and its amazing energies were virtually extensions of him.

McCoy had come to the bridge a few minutes earlier and now stood beside Kirk's chair, watching the main viewing screen with him as Trellisane receded rapidly. The planet dwindled to a point of light, which was joined on the screen by the much brighter point of the system's primary. Both disappeared into the field of stars.

"Warp speed, Captain."

Kirk nodded his acknowledgment.

The first officer left his station and crossed to Kirk's chair, taking up his familiar position on the side opposite to that chosen by McCoy. "Captain," Spock said thoughtfully, "it has occurred to me that under better circumstances Hander Morl could have made a fine Star Fleet officer, perhaps even a ship's captain."

Spock's eyes were on the screen, and he couldn't see the flash of anger that crossed Kirk's face, then quickly vanished. "How so, Mr. Spock?"

"Considering his lack of training, Captain, he managed the *Enterprise* remarkably well under most difficult conditions."

McCoy, who had caught Kirk's momentary display of annoyance, said, "Why, I believe you're right, Mr. Spock. Trust a Vulcan to see it. Morl was arrogant, ruthless, singleminded, egomaniacal. Yes, Spock, the perfect Star Fleet captain." He turned toward the screen, nodding sagely, feigning unawareness of Kirk's glare.

Kirk rose. "Mr. Sulu, you have the con. Bones, Spock, come with me."

He led them to the conference room. When all three had entered and the door had slid shut behind them, Kirk relaxed his self-control and allowed the anger he had been suppressing ever since his return to Trellisane to come to the surface. "All right, gentlemen," he said, his jaw clenched, "I want to know what you two thought you were doing down there while I was away."

"Captain?" Spock said in a puzzled tone. "I don't understand your question."

"Don't play games with me!" Kirk roared. "I finally regained control of the *Enterprise*, managed to browbeat the Klingons and Romulans into a treaty concerning Trellisane and Sealon, only to find that you and McCoy have drawn up some sort of agreement of your own."

"Jim, that's completely unfair," McCoy said, unable to entirely keep his own temper. "We weren't trying to undercut your authority. Spock accomplished something on Sealon that I think is damned near miraculous, and you should be congratulating him for it. You weren't here, we didn't know what had happened to you or if you were even alive, and we both acted as we thought best in the circumstances. Read what the Star Fleet Manual says about officers 'showing initiative and enterprise when not under direct orders.'" He paused for a moment, then laughed suddenly. "Hell, did you want to amend that to read 'when not under direct orders to do otherwise'?"

Shamefaced, Kirk said, "I suppose I overreacted. Look, I knew at the time that both Karox and Tal signed the agreement I worked out for a tripartite commission because they both thought it would give them control of the system in the end. Neither of them would have willingly given up that idea. They wanted to back out, Karox especially, when we got back to

Trellisane and found that the other Klingon forces in the system had been killed and control was now in the hands of the Sealons. The way you two set things up, the system has achieved real independence. The combination of Sealon aggressiveness and Trellisanian technology and science probably means that the alliance will become a real force in the Galaxy in the near future. Both the Klingons and the Romulans could find themselves threatened. They wanted the Tripartite Commission to have control over the Sealons and the Trellisanians, partly to prevent that very thing from ever happening."

"Sorry if we ruined all that Great Power politicking for you, Jim," McCoy said. "I, for one, think this situation is preferable."

"I'm sure you're right. I apologize to both of you. You understand, of course: it was the tension, even the humiliation, all coming together."

McCoy grinned at him. "Plus, of course, that you wanted to be the one who solved everyone's problems, to make up for having your ship stolen from under your nose, and instead you found that we'd already done most of the work. Captain."

Kirk stared at him, trying to will himself to anger but not succeeding. He gave up the struggle and let his face relax into a smile. "It's a good thing you weren't with me on the *Enterprise*, after all, Bones. You're a marvelous ship's doctor, but you're a lousy diplomat."

"Aye, aye, Captain. I won't argue with that at all."

"Nor would I," Spock said. "May we be excused, Captain? I believe both the doctor and I have much work to do to repair the damage done during the takeover."

"Yes, of course, Mr. Spock." He dismissed them with a wave of his hand and watched them leave. As the door was closing behind them, the speaker on the wall behind Kirk spoke out with Uhura's voice.

"Captain, I have a response from Star Fleet Command to the message you sent them when we left Trefolg."

Kirk had to think for a moment to dredge that one up from his memory. Ah, yes, that had been his message that he was going to Trellisane to investigate the plea for help from that world rather than immediately taking his United Expansion Party prisoners to a starbase. At the time, he had been worried, even without Spock's warning, that he was placing his career in jeopardy. His concern over that had been displaced by much more immediate problems during the subsequent days, but it returned now. He felt his muscles tightening. It had taken Star Fleet Command long enough to respond, as he had thought at the time it would. At the time, he had convinced himself that so long a time would be virtually like eternity, that he could simply not think about it. Now eternity had arrived, and he was surprised at his own tension as he said, "Read it to me, Lieutenant."

"Yes, sir. First they acknowledge receipt of your message, then they say, 'Kirk, do not forget the sensitive location of Trellisane. Investigate the situation, but tread warily and do not antagonize the Klingons. However, do what is necessary to guarantee the independence of Trellisane. J. Potgieter, Rear Admiral.' That's all there is, sir."

"Thank you, Lieutenant. I'll be on the way to the bridge shortly." He knew Potgieter; the man functioned more as a liaison with the diplomatic corps than as a regular staff officer. What a wonderfully noncommittal order: investigate, tread warily, do not antagonize, but do what is necessary to guarantee Trellisane's independence. Kirk laughed aloud with the sudden relief of tension. He would have interpreted that command to mean he was on his own, had it arrived in time. As it was, matters had drawn themselves to a conclusion, and the message really meant that he would be commended for his actions when he returned to a starbase, just as he would have been reprimanded had he failed. Star Fleet Command had decided not to decide after all: Kirk had a free hand, but if he failed to bring things off properly, then the fault would be entirely his. But it had always been that way, from the start of his career, as it was for any other officer in a major command position. Eventually it might give him an ulcer. In the meantime, though, he admitted readily to himself, it made his one of the most exciting and satisfying lives in the Galaxy. Perhaps no one else on the ship would be able to fully understand that. Probably only Tal or Karox could sympathize. His enemies and his colleagues simultaneously. The three of them justified each others' existences. What a wonderful joke that was on Star Fleet Command and the equivalent in the Klingon and Romulan empires!

As they left the conference room, Spock said to McCoy, "By the way, Doctor, I'm sure you're aware that your argument concerning the necessity of common ancestry for cross-fertility is neither correct nor logical. The idea of an ancient race from whom we humanoids are all descended is an hypothesis that has never been proven. The archeological evidence is skimpy and inconclusive. Moreover, your argument was a tautology: two races have recent common ancestors because they are cross-fertile, and they are cross-fertile because they have recent common ancestors. It is fortunate that the fallacy in your words didn't strike the Trellisanians as quickly and forcefully as it did me."

McCoy snorted, which he considered a sufficient dismissal of all that Spock had said. "Don't try to confuse a simple country doctor with that sort of verbiage, Spock. It worked, and that's what counts. And speaking of logic, I noticed that when you arrived back on Trellisane in Matabele's ship, you showed definite pleasure and relief that I was unharmed and had come through the Sealon attacks unscathed. That wasn't logic, at all. You can't fool an old country doctor: it was genuine human feeling I saw peeping out." He held his hand up quickly before the Vulcan could reply. "Wait a minute, I know just what you're going to say—that you were merely expressing your relief that Star Fleet's investment in me was not wasted and that the ship needs my professional services for optimal functioning. Right?"

Spock remained imperturbable. "Not quite, Doctor. What is of most value to the *Enterprise*'s optimal functioning is your country-doctor, anti-technology pose. It's good for ship's morale, since humans have a curious need for someone like you as a means of vicariously expressing their romantic delusions. Any competent medical technician could cure their physical ills as well as you do, but no one but you can do such a good job of playing the court jester."

McCoy opened his mouth to say something biting, then closed it with a snap, turned on his heel, and stalked off down the hallway. Spock watched with a faint hint of a smile.

"Mr. Spock, that was cruel."

He turned to find Christine Chapel standing before him, her expression disapproving. "I heard the last part of your conversation. You shouldn't have said that to him. He's really a very sensitive man."

Spock nodded. "Yes, he is a sensitive man. He's also a remarkable doctor, and the *Enterprise* is fortunate to have him. However, he needs occasional correction. More than that, though, I believe he derives great pleasure from insulting me and having me insult him in return. That is the only way he will allow himself to express affection to a being as alien as I." Aquatic images overwhelmed him momentarily. "Unity through diversity," he murmured. "That is our strength. That is what Hander Morl and his party could not understand, even though his group consisted of alien, diverse creatures. It is our ability to communicate and empathize despite our racial differences that makes the Federation strong and healthy." Somewhat brusquely he added, "Of course it is virtually impossible for anyone but a Vulcan to understand that, because only we, of all the races we know, can perform the mind-meld with beings alien to us. Please excuse me, Nurse Chapel. I am needed on the bridge."

Chapel watched him as he hurried away. "Only a Vulcan," she whispered. This was her first trip outside sickbay since her collapse on the bridge, when the Onctiliians had died. No one else on the *Enterprise*, least of all Spock, knew of her experience, of her union with alien beings on a far deeper level than any Vulcan mind-meld had ever been. And no one else ever would know of it. She had been walking slowly down the corridor because she and the Onctiliians had passed this way together on their way to the bridge. . . . It had helped to calm and soothe her. Unity through diversity: no one, not even a Vulcan, would ever understand that idea as deeply as she did. And she knew she would never really experience it again—not as she had for that one, brief, brilliant moment, that too-short time of love, light, and fulfillment. She sighed and walked on, still shaky.

The door of the conference room opened and Captain Kirk came out. Yes, he was back in control and everything was once again where it should be in his private universe, but one thing still rankled, and that was Dr. McCoy's depiction of the perfect starship captain as "arrogant, ruthless, singleminded, egomaniacal." Kirk could not put those words from his mind. Was that what it took, really? Was he that way? Or am I less than perfect? he asked himself with self-conscious irony.

He walked slowly toward the turboelevator entrance, entered, and said, "Bridge." As the elevator sped toward the control center of the *Enterprise*, Kirk returned to the question. Was it arrogant to be aware that he was the best qualified of anyone to command this great ship and its diverse crew? Or ruthless to expect his orders to be obeyed because he was the captain and knew what was best? Or singleminded to be more concerned with this magnificent vessel's well-being than with anything else, including his own well-being? Egomaniacal? "Say that again, Bones," he said aloud, "and I'll have you drawn and quartered." He chuckled.

The doors opened and the bridge lay before him. He could sense the air of—not tension, but extra alertness as he appeared, as if everyone was suddenly concerned to be on his best behavior now that James Kirk was present. Was it egomaniacal to feel more than faintly pleased at that response? he asked himself. Yes, he answered, it is. But he felt no less pleased as he strode toward the chair to resume control of the *Enterprise*.

The Novel STAR TREK® Fans
Have Waited Twenty Years For . . .

STAR TREK®

SPOCK'S WORLD

by
Diane Duane

Ever since 1966, when the very first episode of
the original STAR TREK television series aired,
casual fans and devoted Trekkers alike have been
captivated by the alien Mr. Spock and his home
planet Vulcan.

Now, for the first time anywhere, you can have
an in-depth look at both.

SPOCK'S WORLD...
A September 1988 Hardcover Release
from Pocket Books.